Ira K. Batchelder

Reunion Celebration

together with an historical sketch of Peru, Bennington County, Vermont, and its

inhabitants from the first settlement of the town

Ira K. Batchelder

Reunion Celebration
together with an historical sketch of Peru, Bennington County, Vermont, and its inhabitants
from the first settlement of the town

ISBN/EAN: 9783337383077

Printed in Europe, USA, Canada, Australia, Japan

Cover: Foto ©Andreas Hilbeck / pixelio.de

More available books at **www.hansebooks.com**

OF

PERU,

BENNINGTON COUNTY, VERMONT,

AND

ITS INHABITANTS FROM THE FIRST SETTLEMENT OF THE TOWN.

BY IRA K. BATCHELDER.

BRATTLEBORO:
PHŒNIX JOB PRINT E. L. HILDRETH & CO,
1891.

PREFACE.

At the Centennial Celebration of the settlement of Peru, or reunion of her sons and daughters, they were of the opinion that the town had a history worth preserving, and the very complete historical paper read on that occasion by Hon. Ira K. Batchelder suggested him as the proper person to prepare it. A resident of the town for most of his life, well acquainted with nearly all the early settlers, and prominent in its affairs for half a century, no one among the number was so well equipped for the work as he. After considerable persuasion, Judge Batchelder consented, and the following History of Peru is the result. A great deal of time has been spent in gathering the facts for which Mr. Batchelder receives no remuneration except the gratitude of his former townspeople and those who shall come after, which we are sure he will receive in large measure. In some respects it is not as full as he would have been pleased to have made it, and some families may have been omitted, or mentioned very briefly where a longer account would have been desirable, but this is the common fault of all such histories, where the money received for the sale of the book will not admit of a lengthy work. For this reason the interesting papers read by Hon. James M. Dudley and Dr. Asa Bigelow at the reunion are not inserted. In part they would have been a repetition of what Mr. Batchelder has written. As he very modestly omits all mention of his own family, the lack is partially supplied by the brief notice printed under the head of Biographies.

D. K. SIMONDS.

FAMILIES.

BIOGRAPHIES.

FOURTH OF JULY REUNION.

— ••• —

DEAR SIR: The citizens of Peru have made arrangements for a grand reunion on July 4th, 1870, to which you are cordially invited. It is expected that many of the old residents who have removed to other localities will be present and it is desirable to have as many join with us on that occasion as possible. The exercises will consist of

AN ORATION
BY
HON. JAMES M. DUDLEY,
OF JOHNSTOWN, N. Y.

A HISTORICAL ADDRESS
BY
HON. IRA K. BATCHELDER,
OF TOWNSHEND, VT.

A POEM
BY
HON. D. K. SIMONDS,
OF MANCHESTER, VT.

There will also be a dinner with
TOASTS AND RESPONSES.

If you decide to come please reply to that effect as soon as convenient.

ROBERT I. BATCHELDER,
For Committee.

Peru, Vt., June 2d, 1870.

The above invitation was sent to all resident and non-resident citizens and friends, who made a generous response, saying they would be present to unite with residents and friends of their native home in the festivities of the day, to rejoice with friends who had been so long separated by time and distance, and to breathe the pure air and drink of the sparkling water of their native hills on the Green mountains.

Among the responses to be present is the following, which I insert to remind us of David:

Londonderry, Vt., June 11, 1879.

To Robert I. Batchelder and Committee of Invitation of the Reunion at Peru, July 4. 1879.

Dear Sir and Friends: We, mother of the original stock, David a limb of the same, Samuel Dudley and his broods, distinguished company far fetched, Carrie and Molly and broods, all limbs and sprouts of Peru stock; and George J., L. A., and F. Arnold Starbuck from a distance may be, and will endeavor to be on hand, and perhaps a city lawyer from New York, branches and limbs as aforesaid.

Very respectfully yours,

DAVID ARNOLD.

Also the following from Mrs. Lucy Gray, formerly Lucy Simonds:

Dekalb, Ill., June 24, 1879.

MR. ROBERT I. BATCHELDER.

Dear Sir: I received your kind invitation to be present at the reunion of old settlers at your place on the Fourth. I assure you that it would be highly gratifying to me to be present and see the home of my childhood, and renew the associations I once enjoyed, but age and infirmity prevent. I am in my eighty-second year, and will have to content myself in the far off region of the West. I know when that day comes my thoughts will go back to my old home in the East, and will be present in spirit though not in form. May it be a good day to all of you and not without profit, and I do rejoice that our country is free.

Yours with respect,

MRS. LUCY GRAY.

Many responded by writing who could not be present in person, but said they should be present in spirit, and sent their congratulations to all present with good-will and love.

THE MANCHESTER JOURNAL'S ACCOUNT OF THE REUNION:

Not less than three thousand people attended the reunion celebration the 4th, two hundred of whom were old residents, most of the old families being represented. Of the Bigelow family, Dr. Asa Bigelow, of Toledo, Ohio, Mrs. Fairchild, of Wisconsin, and Mrs. Dr. Whiting, of Chester; of the Warren family, Rev. S. Mills Warren, of Roxbury, Mass., and Herbert Marshall Warren; of the Dudley family, Hon. J. M. Dudley, of Johnstown, N. Y., Mrs. David Arnold and Mrs. Jesse Rider, of Londonderry, and Mrs. Curtis, of Hoosick, N. Y.; of the Barnard family, Luke and Seth Barnard, and

Mrs. Haynes, of Wilmington, Charles Barnard, of Illinois, Mrs. I. K. Batchelder, of Townshend, Mrs. J. J. Hapgood, of Cambridge, Mass., Mrs. Eviline Whitney, of Glens Falls, Mrs. Eleanor Gillson, of Chester, Mrs. Lydia Allen, of Greenfield, Mass., Mrs. Emma Dutton, Mrs. F. P. Batchelder, of Ludlow; of the Batchelder family, Hon. Ira K. Batchelder and Edward Batchelder, of Townshend, Edward and John L. Batchelder, Mrs. Ira Cochran and Mrs. D. L. Kent, of Dorset, F. P. Batchelder, of Ludlow, J. G. Batchelder, of Wilmington, and Jas. K. Batchelder, of Arlington; of the Lyon family, Charles Lyon, of Shushan, N. Y., and H. M. Lyon, of Massachusetts; of the Burton family, Dr. R. B. Burton, of New York City, Mrs. Charles Lyon, of Shushan, N. Y., and Mrs. A. J. Gray, of Manchester; of the Hapgood family, L. B. Hapgood and Miss Charlotte Hapgood, of Cambridge, Mass., and Charles Hapgood, of Easton, Pa.; of the Simonds family, S. D. Simonds, of Illinois, Oscar Simonds, of Pennsylvania, Mrs. A. F. Clark, of Leverett, Mass., Mrs. L. Howe, of Brattleboro, and Mrs. Simpson of Hoosick, N. Y. There were many more old residents present, some of whom we did not see, but we mention the above as fair specimens of those present and to show that the reunion was a success. Besides old residents there was a large crowd of people present from neighboring towns. The procession was formed under the direction of Geo. K. Davis, Esq., marshal, at 10 a. m., and reached from the village to the grove, as closely packed as an ordinary road would allow. The exercises at the grove were opened by Dexter Batchelder, Esq., president of the day, who welcomed the guests in a few fitting words, and introduced Rev. A. F. Clark, who was for many years pastor of the Congregational church, who offered prayer. Hon. James M. Dudley, orator of the day, was next introduced, and spoke for nearly an hour, his address being very appropriate to the occasion, well written and well delivered, and it was received by the audience with many tokens of approval. His references to incidents and events in the early history of the town moved the audience, especially the old residents, sometimes to laughter, sometimes to tears. Hon. Ira K. Batchelder followed with an historical sketch which included the early settlement of the town, with an extended account of all the prominent families. After speaking half an hour signs of rain caused an adjournment to the church, where Mr. Batchelder finished, occupying nearly two hours in all. The history must have cost a vast amount of labor and was very interesting, especially to old residents. This was followed by dinner, which was furnished by the residents, and fully sustained their enviable reputation for deeds of hospitality. The shower somewhat interfered with the culinary arrangements, but did not spoil a good dinner nor prevent its thorough appreciation by the hungry guests. After dinner the exercises were resumed in the church, opened by a poem by D. K. Simonds, which appeared to be well received. Dr. Asa Bigelow followed with a short address containing many amusing reminiscences, especially interesting to the older persons present. This was followed by the following sentiments and responses under the direction of J. B. Simonds, who acted as toastmaster. The day we celebrate; response by the Londonderry Cornet Band. The ladies of Peru; responded to by D. K. Simonds. Peru: May the moral character of its people be as high and prominent as its mountains; responded to by Rev. Asa F. Clark. The home of our childhood; response by a vocal trio, "Home Again Returning." Vermont: May its institutions of learning and the religious character of its people be everlasting; responded to by Hon. A. L. Miner. May there be many happy returns of the day to all present; response by the Weston Cornet Band. Peru: A good place to raise lawyers, but too elevated to support them; responded to by J. K. Batchelder. The family: The foundation of State, may its influence in Peru be preserved pure and intelligent; responded to by Samuel M. Warren. Morality from religious principles the foundation of true manhood; responded to by Rev. R. D. Miller. Education: May our young people ever prize it above all other gifts; response by Ira K. Batchelder. Our old families; responded to by James M. Dudley. Our children at home: May they keep the fires burning brightly in order to welcome back the friends of "Auld Lang Syne;" responded by M. J. Hapgood. Should auld acquaintance be forgot; response by all singing, "Auld Lang Syne." The responses were all appropriate and added much to the interest of the occasion. Almost every speaker during the day feelingly referred to the high character of the old residents of the town who have passed away, and testified to their appreciation of the old Puritan influences under which they were brought up. It was five o'clock before the speaking was finished, and some of the visitors were so much interested in the occasion that they would have prolonged the meeting far into the night if left to themselves. The showers during the day made it very unpleasant for those who could not find room in the church, and no doubt some went home disgusted, but the rain could not be helped, and but for that the celebration would have been satisfactory to everybody. The citizens of Peru did everything possible to make the occasion pleasant and one long to be remembered by those present. The Londonderry and Weston Cornet Bands made plenty of excellent music and added much to the interest of the occasion. The latter band has been organized but a short time, but played very nicely, and with more practice can become one of the best bands in the State. The Londonderry Band has already gained a good reputation, which they fully sustained on this occasion. After the celebration the Londonderry Band serenaded Mrs. Anna Simonds, who is eighty-eight years old, and was not able to be present at the celebration. Among the pleasant incidents of the occasion was the contribution of a purse of one hundred dollars to the Peru Congregational Society by friends from abroad, to assist in repairs on the church and parsonage. A movement was also made for printing a complete history of the town, and a committee, composed of Ira K. Batchelder, D. K. Simonds and M. J. Hapgood, was appointed to take such steps as may be necessary to attain that object. We would be very glad to publish in the JOURNAL the orations, etc., in full, but our limited space forbids. If the proposed history is published no doubt they will be included in that work.

The following letter, which has been received by the Committee of Invitation of the Peru reunion, expresses the sentiments of nearly all the guests.

New York, July 8, 1879.

To R. I. Batchelder and others:

Dear Sir: The charming retrospect of that reunion is so charming that I cannot refrain from expressing my great thanks to you for your invitation, and to all others concerned. It seems as if all the arrangements from first to last were planned by inspiration. The selection of orator, historian and poet was faultless. The music and all of the subsequent exercises were carried on with the best possible effect. The dinner was good and your hospitality was boundless. If Peru has decreased in population it surely has not in the quality of what is left. I think really only one such event can happen in our lifetime, but I rejoice to think that we can carry the remembrance of it to our last moments.

Very respectfully,

DR. R. B. BURTON.

THE POEM.

Great times we have at our house, the boys are on their way
To visit the old homestead on Independence Day,
And their sisters and cousins and aunts, and the Lord only knows who
Will be here that day to join in the mighty hullabaloo,
And Sarah Jane and I have been as busy as a bee
In putting everything to rights for the boys and girls to see.
We are bound they shan't go hungry, we know they'll not be sad,
For haven't we worked like beavers to make their coming glad.
Our house is filled with good things, pies, puddings, pork and beans,
Ham, turkey, chicken fixins, and well, I think there's greens;
Doughnuts? Yes, there's doughnuts, you can bet your life on that,
For Sarah Jane, she fried a cart load and used up all the fat.
Last night I killed the fatted calf, the prodigal is sure to come,
And I wa'nt that when he gets here, he'll find the folks at home.
'Tis true we're getting rather old, good Sarah Jane and I,
But if you'd seen us fixing up you'd thought us dreadful spry,
For everything about the house was getting rather slack
And it really makes us young again to have the boys come back.
Mother's afraid they'll be stuck up and put on city airs,
But if they're a mind to be such fools I'd like to know who cares.
'Tis true most all have done quite well and some have done first rate,
But they will leave their stuck up airs outside the front yard gate;
Of course they know we're homespun folks that never put on style
And won't expect kid gloves and sich in tillers of the "sile,'"
How I would feel in stovepipe hat and shiny broadcloth suit,
And mother in a damask silk with frills and lace to boot!
You might as well hitch up a cow and put her in a gig,
And speed her on a trotting course, as to put us in such rig.
But when you come to honest toil, though we are past our prime,
A working in the house or field, you'll find us every time;
And the boys will never fail to find a welcome kind and true
Whenever they see fit to come away up to Peru.
But bless me how they're scattered, from Maine to Iowa;
They've gone to seek their fortins and bound to make it pay.
But then it is no wonder, whether we won't or will,
We know that men, like water, are bound to run down hill.
The water from Old Bromley runs north, south, east and west,
And so our sons and daughters take which course each likes best;
They surely can't go higher up, unless in a balloon,
And even they will hardly try a journey to the moon.
But we will trust these boys of ours, for don't we surely know
That they will show their bringing up no matter where they go;
And they were never taught at home to cheat and steal and lie,
Nor loaf around bad whiskey shops, or drinking on the sly;
But they were all brought up to work and earn their daily bread,

To rise not later than the sun, and with the sun to bed.
I know it seems a little hard, but then they had their fun,
And all the sweeter, too, for them, with all their labor done;
Such boys we know will make their mark, and never bring disgrace
Upon the man who brought them up or on their native place.
You'll pardon me for words of praise, indeed I can't do less
Than tell the truth behind their backs, and that won't hurt I guess;
The world has need of just such boys in every spot and place,
They'll all pull true, and never balk or stumble in the race.
But I must tell you about the boys we expect to see,
A better lot you'd seldom find beneath a family tree;
There's Jim we sent away to school because he would not work,
And every time the job was hard he'd always try to shirk,
He studied law, of course he did, the law's the place for him,
But who'd a thought they'd ever made a judge of lazy Jim?
There's Ira K., he bought a farm and worked it very well,
And always raised enough to eat, with plenty left to sell,
And so he got a little proud and thought he'd rather go
Where people have more rocks and where there is less snow;
And so he went, but quickly found though snow is pesky stuff
That water, too, is rather bad when one has more'n enough.
Then there's D. K., we always thought he'd come to some bad end,
For every cent that he could get he'd find a way to spend;
He went to school and studied law, but never made much stir,
And now he's settled down into a country editor.
I quite forgot, he's been gone so long, to mention Asa B.,
Though he was jolly when he was young and dearly loved a spree;
And then there's another Asa B., whom all of you must know,
He's rather high, although you see his name is Bige*low;*
And Moody, too, who stayed at home till he was eighty-one,
Before he went across the hill to have a little fun;
And Wot, a hard-working boy and always full of pluck,
But somehow things would not go right, he never had no luck,
And Asa F., who used to preach, and tried to practice too,
Which is a great deal better than, I fear, some preachers do;
There's Luke and Charles and Seth, three honest boys and true,
Who manage to save their coppers and a little silver too;
Charles he went to Illinois, and thinks he hit the mark,
For farming there is easier than peeling hemlock bark.
Ed and John did not go far before the critters found
What proved to be a very good opening -in the ground.
They did not go quite far enough to be rid of Vermont rocks,
But the kind they have is very good and always raised in blocks.
Then there's Luke B., a merchant prince, at least he might have been
If he had staid in the old store and settled down his tin,
But he must go and try his hand way down in big Boston,
And now, though he may have less cash perhaps he has more fun;

And there's James K., a lawyer, too, of good ability,
Whether you lose or win your case, he'll never lose the fee;
But then you hardly ever see, at least I never saw
A man who got exceedingly rich by always going to law.
And then there's Oscar, who will come from Pennsylvania,
Who has found, it seems, that even there life is not all child's play,
But he has done his very best to help his fellow men
By trying to support his wife, also his children ten;
There's Elb, who used when he was young, to flirt with all the girls,
And always sure to lose his head at sight of pretty curls;
But long ago he steadied down and sticks to work I suppose,
For marriage is a sure cure for all such freaks as those.
And then John G., a jolly boy and always full of fun,
And every chance that he could get to Landgrove he would run;
And Samuel M., who used to be clear up above them all,
For he lived *high*, I don't mean fast, nor extremely tall.
And Mahlon too, an honest boy, a lover of his books,
A doctor now, though one would hardly think it from his looks;
And there is Charles, a curious boy, who likes it seems, a span,
And is, as everybody knows, a stiff cold water man.
And Porter J., who left his farm, but still we all agree
That he will make, if he keeps on, a first rate deputy;
And Aiden, a rather puny boy and slender of his age,
Who expects to be a conductor on the narrow guage;
Aiden he will sure be here, his senses in a whirl,
For he, like any good young man will bring along his girl.
And others too we shall expect, while others cannot come,
Though we would like right well to see all the boys at home.
Now I've thus far only told you of the boys who roam,
But I must also say a word of those who staid at home;
Some good, some bad, but on the whole I think they will compare
In every good and honest work with boys raised anywhere.
There's Tom, my eldest, always stiddy, never shirked his meals,
And still he's happy, though old age, like twilight, o'er him steals;
And Frank, a very steady worker, and always hearty too,
And never really, truly happy without a heap to do;
And Edmund, another stiddy boy, whom we always knew
Would be a deacon if he lived, a very good deacon too,
And while I'm on the deacon list I must not skip O. P.,
Who always would stick to the last like bark unto a tree.
And then there's Deck, a jolly boy, who rather likes his ease,
But makes a living off his farm, and sometimes he makes cheese;
There's John, Ide and Seth, and also Merrill G.,
If they should go away from home they'd sure to be all at sea,
And Jonathan sticks tight at home and minds his little biz,
And hardly comes to town to find out whether butter's riz.
There's Harvey S. and Kiah, too, now better boys are scarce,

And girls who ketch and marry them might do a great deal worse;
And John, but he is caught at last, indeed we know he's gone,
A pretty girl just smiled on him, and then 'twas goodbye John.
I need not tell you of Geo. K., of course you know him well,
He's one of those who just know how to keep a good hotel;
Then there's Mark B., Clark J., and others too, but I have said enough,
And fear you'll think what I have said is naught but silly stuff.
I'd like to tell you of our girls, of whom we raised a crop,
But should I get to praising them I fear I'd never stop,
But you'll soon see what *they* can do, in fact they can't be beat
In getting up a rousing meal for hungry folks to eat;
And now I think you've heard enough about our family,
And if you ever come to town, drop in, and stay to tea.

D. K. SIMONDS.

ATTRACTIONS OF PERU.

As to the scenery, let him judge of it who has ever crossed the mountain upon the turnpike from Manchester. As he rounds the top, suddenly there bursts upon the view a sight which no one whose heart is at all akin to nature can ever forget. Stretched in full glory below him lies the whole broad valley of the upper West River and its tributaries, while beyond the vision follows range after range, and is lost only amid the giants of the White Mountains. But by far dearer to me is the journey across the Notch. As you reach the top, the eye rests upon a broad stretch of wilderness, extending for miles in every direction. Half way down, where a half dozen brooks gather, I have camped each year for weeks at a time. No sound, save the rustle of a leaf and the rush of the mad, leaping waters, with an atmosphere wafted into the face such as kings or emperors, in their gorgeous palaces, never breathe. I take my rod, I fish for miles, north, south, east or west. I cross no clearing and pass over no boundary line. I follow the main branch, which is the head-waters of the Battenkill, two miles to the north, cross a slight ridge, alight upon the head-waters of the Otter Creek, fish it down another two miles, until I arrive at that incomparable sheet of water, Buffom Pond. All of this time I have been traveling due north, and have not left the bounds of my native town, or been within two miles of a clearing. I might have gone south with nearly the same result. When I reach Buffom, *I am there!* Where?—in Paradise, or as near Paradise as I can well get on earth. Time and again I have traveled the Adirondacks, but there is nothing there in that magnificent region to surpass it. With a hard, stony shore and bottom, all around is the virgin forest, as yet unpolluted by the hand of man. The heavy, dense fir trees crowd in on all sides in the vain endeavor to fill the watery space. You shout, and the woods echo and re-echo your voice until it reaches the mountains

that surround you upon all sides, but no ear, save the ear of the
sportsman, catches the sound. Everywhere is nature, just as the
Creator made it, wild, strong, full, running over, romantic!

One cannot stay here but a short time and not get hungry. Yet
don't get alarmed, friend, or bring in with you your stale cooked
provender. Nature has made ample provision. In those deep, still
waters floats meat fit for the gods, and such, I ween, as the gods
very seldom get, rich, fire red, just large enough to spin the reel and
set the nerves all a quiver as you draw them out, these speckled,
smooth skinned beauties are ahead of anything which Jay Gould
can purchase with his two hundred millions. For over twenty years
I have visited this region annually, and never yet failed to get my
fill, and only those who have been with me can have any idea,
whatever, what that means. And I can truthfully boast of sport
obtained right here in my native state, unique, unexcelled, even by
your Maine or Canadian professional. Standing upon a well
balanced raft, and moored in water twenty feet deep, four times in
succession I have hooked with my seven ounce rod three trout at a
time, weighing from four to sixteen ounces each; at the last cast the
fourth hook was taken by a sixteen ounce bull head. I have
followed up a wild stream, unfished since I left it the year before,
stood at the foot of a round basin ten feet across, and laid out, one
by one, upon the bank, as my wife cast them quivering towards me,
twenty-seven plump, fat, *legal* trout. For nearly a week at a time I
have camped, with ladies, in the heart of this wilderness, with only
the ground for a floor and a bark roof, all open in front, for a cover;
and carried in hardly more than a single loaf of cooked food. I
have myself put upon the bark table, steaming hot, ready for
simultaneous consumption, well cooked trout, pork, pancakes,
potatoes, maple syrup and coffee. Well, you only who have been
there know what it means, with only the open fire to cook over.
Outsiders can have no more idea of it than a crocodile has of music.
Often I have gone for months without a meal of victuals, although I
have one of the best cooks in the parts at the head of my household.
I go through the ceremony of eating, and manage to dispose of a
large amount of fodder, yet only when I get back to the old camp
and come in after a hard day's tramp, with fire to kindle, trout to
dress, and supper to get, with its aroma tantalizing my nostrils, do I
feel like *eating?* But mind one thing, some one else washes the
dishes, or else they go until morning.

"And now comes still evening on,
    And twilight, grey,
Has in her sober livery, all things clad."

" The other member of the party" throws fresh fuel upon the camp fire. The woods around glimmer with the wavering light. Fantastic shadows dance hither and thither. High overhead the paled stars shine dimly out. Somehow I manage to move a little to where the balsam boughs lie in thick profusion under the projecting bark. Some kind, considerate friend hands me a cigar. Slowly, calmly, fully I taste the fragrant weed, and watch the wreaths of smoke as they curl gracefully up. That most important of all events, viz: digestion, is, undoubtedly, now taking place. I feel at peace with all mankind and all creation. I doubt whether, if that most hated of all enemies, the mosquito, should now alight upon me that I should raise a hand to crush it. Even though he who nominated me as church committee, should now look upon me, I think that I should smile upon him. But hark! What sound is that, repeated at long, full intervals? Ah, comrades! You have fallen, fallen ignominiously, without a struggle. Well, sleep—the best, strongest, sweetest, most health-giving sleep known to mortal, is yours. The fire will soon die out, yet the stars will grow brighter and watch over you. Soon the full orbed moon will start in her course westward across the sky. No nightmare, no dreams even, will be yours. And in the morning the scent of the balsam will be in your clothes. Your hands will rub it into your eyes, and melting dew will carry it everywhere through the air. Not even a plunge into the cold, pure water, will wash it away. Ah me! As I sit at my desk at mid-winter, I can live over again the only real, true part of my life.

Yes, I am fully convinced that no other place in these parts offers equal attractions for the tired and dejected denizens of our cities who seek rest, recreation and quiet. We have a telegraph line and a daily mail from each direction; and a landlord whose tables even now millionaires drive miles out of their way to enjoy. No description of our town would be at all complete without mention of our honored host, Mr. G. K. Davis, whose name shall fittingly close our wayward description.

                                            M. J. HAPGOOD.

HISTORY OF PERU.

The history of a small country town, and that in no way conspicuous among its neighbors, can hardly be expected to furnish much to interest the general reader. Such a work must be made up of particulars and minute details. It is seldom that great or distinguished characters occur to give interest to the story. The narrative must derive its claim to the reader's attention mainly from his acquaintance with the scenes, or his connection with the actors described. The problem of history may be thus stated, giving the present state, condition and character of the people, to determine those influences in the past which have tended to produce these results. It is the task of the historian to trace the development of these influences and so to arrange the history of events as to give a miniature of the character and spirit of the age which he describes. He must set before us not only the great statesmen and scholars, but also ordinary men in their ordinary dress, and engaged in their ordinary employment. He must visit the dwellings of the poor and the abodes of misery as well as the palaces of wealth and luxury. No anecdote, no familiar saying is insignificant which can throw light upon the state of education, morals or religion, or mark the progress of the human mind. Since the natural features of a country have an important influence upon the character of its inhabitants, they must be described in their primitive wildness as well as in their present state of cultivation and improvements.

CHARTER

AND DOINGS OF THE ORIGINAL PROPRIETORS.

Peru lies in the northeast corner of Bennington county, bounded on the north by Mount Tabor, east by Landgrove, south by Winhall, west by Dorset. It was chartered at Portsmouth,

N. H., by Benning Wentworth, October 13th, 1761, as colonial
governor of the Province of New Hampshire, receiving his
appointment from King George the Third, by the name of
Bromley, for the due encouragement of settling a new plantation
within said province under certain reservations and conditions.

PROVINCE OF NEW HAMPSHIRE.

I, George the Third, By the Grace of God of Great Britain,
France and Ireland, Defender of the Faith. To all to whom these
presents shall come: For the encouragement of settling a new
plantation within our State Province by and with the advice of
our trusty and well beloved Friend, Benning Wentworth, Our
Governor and Commander-in-Chief of our Province of New
Hampshire and of our council of said Province, Upon the
conditions and reservations hereinafter made, given and granted,
and by these presents for us and our heirs and successors, do give
and grant in equal shares unto our loving subjects, inhabitants of
our said Province and our other governments, to their heirs and
assigns forever, Whose names are entered on this grant to be
divided among them into 72 equal shares all that tract or parcel
of Land situate lying and being within our said Province, containing
23,040 acres, according to a plan and survey made by our
Governor's order and returned into our Secretary's office, butted
and bounded as follows, Viz., Beginning at the northwest corner of
Winhall, Thence due north six miles to the southwest corner of
Harwich (Mt. Tabor), Thence east six miles to the southeast
corner thereof, Thence due south six miles to the northeast corner
of Winhall, Thence due west by Winhall to bounds began at, and
the same is incorporated into a Township by the name of Bromley,
and the inhabitants that do or shall hereafter inhabit said Township
are enfranchised with and entitled to all the privileges that other
towns exercise and enjoy, and as soon as there shall be fifty families
residing and settled thereon, they shall have the liberty of holding
two fairs, and a market may be opened one or two days in a week,
and the first meeting for choice of Town Officers agreeable to the
laws of our Province shall be held on the first Monday of
November next; said meeting shall be notified by Samuel Gilbert,
and the annual meetings for the choice of Town Officers shall be
held on the second Tuesday of March annually. To have and to
hold said tract with the appurtenances thereof to them and their
heirs and assigns forever upon the following conditions:

1. Every grantee, his heirs or assigns, shall plant and cultivate five acres of land for every 50 acres owned, and shall continue to do so upon penalty of forfeiting his grant of said Township.

2. All white or pine trees suitable for masting our Royal Navy shall be carefully preserved for that use.

3. Before any division of said land shall be made among the grantees, a grant of land as near the centre of the Township as may be, one acre of Land allotted to each grantee for a Town Lot.

4. Yielding and paying to us, our heirs or successors, one ear of Indian corn on the 25th day of December for ten years.

5. Every proprietor settling or inhabitating shall yield or pay unto us, our heirs and successors on and after the 25th day of December, 1772, one shilling, proclamation money, to any officer appointed to receive the same.

There is no record of any proprietors' meeting until 1797. A meeting of the proprietors was called by the request of the proprietors by Moses Warnér, Justice of the Peace of Andover, to be held at the Inn of Jonathan Butterfield in Bromley the 2nd day of March, 1797. Proprietors met agreeable to warning. Chose Joseph Bullard, Moderator; Ebenezer Hurlburt, Proprietors' Clerk; Joseph Bullard, Treasurer; John Waters, Collector. Chose a committee of three, consisting of Nathaniel Leonard, Benjamin W. Willard and John Waters, instructed them to run the out lines of Bromley. Voted that persons who have made pitches and improved and built on them, be quieted, have them instead of their lot; if they had any legal title to a right. Voted the committee be instructed to lay out and survey three lots of one hundred acres to each proprietor's right, to be numbered first, second, and third division of said right, and to be drawn separately. The record of said division and draft is found on the 80th page of proprietors' record and onward. The whole expense of surveying, according to the above record, was $917.63. At a proprietors' meeting held June 6, 1798, voted that $13.90 should be assessed to each proprietor's right, to be collected and paid into the treasury before the 7th inst.

The meetings of the proprietors were kept alive by adjournment from time to time, year after year. September 6th, 1798, adjourned June 5th, 1799; then adjourned to September 10th, 1800, A. D. Chose Reuben Bigelow, Proprietors' Clerk, Bromley, September 10th, 1800. Meeting opened according to adjournment. Chose a committee of Ebenezer Hurlburt, Esquire Kimball of Harvard, and

Reuben Bigelow to be empowered in behalf of the proprietors to
treat with Asa Utley and others respecting the land in the east part
of Bromley, which Utley and others pretended to claim. It is said
and thought that the Utleys, who were the first settlers, found the
east and west lines were over six miles, allowance having been made
for the high mountains which lay in the west part of the town.
Utley made the east line further west than the original survey,
claiming the land as a part of the gore now Landgrove. Several
law suits grew out of it, and it was finally settled by the Legislature
establishing a jurisdictional line in 1835. Also said committee to
prosecute Asa Utley and others or defend to final judgment any
suit which may be brought or commenced respecting this land.
Voted to dissolve this meeting; Attest R. Bigelow, Proprietors'
Clerk. Reuben Bigelow defended suit brought by Asa Utley and
others against the proprietors of Bromley. His bill for the same
was $283.88, which amount was allowed by the proprietors the 29th
day of September, 1802. By request of more than one-tenth of the
proprietors a meeting was warned to be holden at the house of
Reuben Bigelow the 29th day of September, 1802, by Robert
Pierpoint, Justice of the Peace. Meeting called by Proprietors'
Clerk. Voted to assess each right $4.17 to pay expense of law suit.
Proprietors' meetings were held and adjourned each year until 1809.
Another law suit was had between Asa Utley and others and the
proprietors of Bromley in regard to the disputed land in the easterly
part of the town. No settlement was effected. The proprietors had
to pay a bill of cost amounting to $341.22. At a meeting held by
the proprietors September 14th, 1809, they voted to raise a tax on
each right of individual land of $5.17, which was raised and paid.
At a meeting of the proprietors held September 3rd, 1815, a
committee of two from each town of Landgrove and Peru, who had
been appointed, made a report establishing the line surveyed by
Esquire Dunton in part, and completed by Daniel Ormsby, county
surveyors, A. D. 1803. Report dated January 3rd, 1814. Jonathan
Twist, Nathan Burton, committee for Peru; Asa Utley, Peabody
Utley, committee for Landgrove. The report was accepted by
the proprietors at a meeting of the proprietors. At a subsequent
meeting the acceptance was reconsidered; no settlement was effected
under the proprietors' administration. The disputed land in the
easterly part of the town without further suits for the soil. A
pauper suit grew out of it. After one or two suits was settled

DEA. JOHN BATCHELDER

another generation occupying the land, old feuds and quarrels are forgotten. Peter Dudley and Josiah Barnard were elected a committee to lay out and survey a fourth division of lots on the undivided land. In their report they reported 15 acres were divided to each proprietor's right. Johnson Marsh, Surveyor; expenses of the same, $58.50. September 24th, 1824, meeting adjourned to the 2nd Wednesday in September next. No record of another proprietors' meeting until May 15th, 1853. A meeting of the proprietors was warned to meet at L. Howard's hotel in Peru on the 14th day of July, 1853, by Welcome Allen, Justice of the Peace. Peru, July 14th, 1853, proprietors met agreeably to above warrant. Chose O. P. Simonds, Moderator; O. P. Simonds, Proprietors' Clerk; Johnson Marsh, Collector; George Marsh, Treasurer. Voted to make a fifth division of all the undivided land in Peru. Chose Johnson Marsh committee to allot said land by employing a surveyor and other help necessary to do it. Voted that said division and survey be completed and presented to proprietors at L. Howard's hotel in Peru on the 30th day of November next, at one o'clock p. m. At Peru, November 30th, 1853, at the hotel of L. Howard, Johnson Marsh, committee to allot and survey the undivided land in Peru, reported he had performed the duties and divided said land into 32 acre lots, and made a draft for each proprietor's share. Voted to accept the above report as valid and correct. Cost of the survey and division, $96.63. Annual meeting of the proprietors was held by adjournment until May 21st, 1857, A. D. No record of any further meeting of the proprietors can be found.

This last and final division was of the land on the west mountain, south of the notch road, being east of Dorset east line.

The Colonial Governor of the Colony of New York, in his surveys on New Hampshire Grants, surveyed all the territory embracing Peru, giving it the name of Brindley. It is not known that he granted it to any individual or chartered it to any number of individuals, and no person ever claimed title under a grant from New York officials.

I am indebted to Judge Wheeler, who furnished me with these facts, and who has a plot of Brindley in connection with adjacent towns. It is found in the documentary history of New York at Albany. I presume this survey of the New York Governor was subsequent to the charter granted by Governor Wentworth in 1761.

FIRST KNOWN WHITE PERSONS IN TOWN.

The first white men who trod on the soil of Peru were a company of eighteen men under command of Captain Eleazer Melvin, who started from Northfield, Mass., on the 13th day of May, 1748, on an expedition against the Indians on or about Lake Champlain. The record of the journey says:

"Marched the first day to No. 2, camped; May 14th, they marched to No. 4; from No. 4 (Charlestown) marched northwesterly over the mountains to the Lake. On May 25th fired at the Indians from a point about a mile from Crown Point. The Indians being so numerous they retreated east three or four miles, thence traveled southeast ten miles, camped; May 26th, marched southeast about five miles, south about eleven miles further; May 27th, marched southeast to Otter Creek, one mile below the first falls, and marched about four miles above the falls; May 28th, marched up Otter Creek to the Crotch, about six miles, up south branch ten miles; May 29th, marched up the south branch to the head of it, thence southeast over a large mountain, leaving another large mountain on the northwest, keeping course down the mountain, crossed several streams supposed to be the head waters of Saratoga River (now Battenkill), marched this day about sixteen miles; May 30th, marched south southeast about six miles, came upon a branch of West River, traveled down the river about eight miles, camped; May 31st, our provisions being very short we began our march before sunrise and traveled till about half-past nine o'clock, being beside the river. Several of the company desired to stop to replenish, being faint and weary, whereupon we halted and began to take off our packs and sat down, and in about a half minute after our halting the enemy rose from behind a log and several trees about twenty or thirty feet at the furthest distance and fired about twelve guns at us, but do not know whether any men received any hurt though so near. Whereupon I called to the men to face the enemy and run up the bank, which I did myself, and several others attempted, but the enemy was so thick they could not. I had no sooner jumped up the bank but the enemy were so thick just upon me I discharged my gun at one of them about eight feet from the muzzel of my gun, who I saw fall about the same time that

ISRAEL BATCHELDER.

I discharged my gun. The enemy fired about twenty guns at us, killed four men, viz.: John Hayward, Isaac Taylor, John Dod and Daniel Man. The men who were alive, or most of them, fired immediately on the enemy, several of which shots did execution, as can be witnessed by several who saw the enemy fall, but seeing the enemy numerous and their guns being discharged, they retreated, several ran across the river, where some of them had a chance, or opportunity, to fire again at the enemy. Some ran up the river and some down, and some into the thicket on the same side of the river. For my own part, after I saw my men retreat, and being beset by the enemy with guns, hatchets and knives, one of which, or a bullet, I cannot certainly tell which, carried away my belt, and with it my bullets, all except one I had loose in my pocket. I ran down the river and two Indians followed almost side by side with me, calling, 'Come, Captain, Now, Captain,' but upon my presenting my gun towards them, though not charged, they fell a little back and ran across the river. I charged my gun, moved a few steps and one of them fired at me, which was the last gun fired. I looked back and saw nine of the enemy scalping the dead men, and six or seven running across the river and several about the bank of the river, all very busy, which I apprehended were carrying off their dead. I then, being alone, went to the side of the hill in sight of the plan of battle, and there seated myself to look for some of my men and to see if the enemy made any shout, as is customary with them when they get the advantage. But hearing no more of them, nor seeing any of my own men, I made the best of my way to Fort Dummer, where I arrived the next day before noon. One of my men got in an hour before me, eleven more came in a few hours in different companies. Six men were killed in the fight. Captain Melvin returned the next day with forty men to bury the dead."

The above was copied from Melvin's Journal, in New Hampshire Historical Collection, Volume 5, pages 109, 110 and 111.

Ensign Taylor was taken captive by the Indians between Hinsdale and Fort Dummer the 17th day of August, 1748. He was taken up West River over the Highlands to the head-waters of Otter Creek. Taylor, on his return from captivity, gave an account of passing over the ground where Captain Melvin's affair happened. There is no doubt but that Captain Melvin's party were the first white persons ever passed through Peru, and Ensign Taylor was taken up West River, passed over the high land to the head-waters of the Otter Creek, through Peru, A. D. 1748, and Indian arrows were found in the sand bed below the Haynes mill about 1825. I am indebted to Judge Wheeler, of Brattleboro, for furnishing these facts. It is an established fact that the Indians, during the time the French owned and occupied Canada, frequently crossed the mountains in their predatory excursions upon the frontier settlements on and east of the Connecticut river, following up the streams to the low places on the mountains, then down the branches that run into the Connecticut river and *vice versa*.

Captain William Utley came from Connecticut with his family in 1769. He settled on the spot where Menzie Thompson's house stands. Undoubtedly he expected and knew that he was in the Township of Bromley; as evidence that he thought so he attended three of the early conventions of the State as delegate from the town of Bromley, viz.: He was a delegate at Dorset in 1776; on October 30th, 1776, was delegate at a session held at Westminster; also delegate at a session held at Windsor, November 9, 1777. It was said the line of the town was east of the Utley house called the Mun line. Bromley being surveyed, more than six miles allowance was made for the high mountain; its being measured from the west line six miles without allowance for the mountain brought the line a half mile or more west of Utley's house, leaving Utley on the gore of land between Weston and Bromley. This was a bone of contention for years. The difficulty was referred to commissioners at different times, but no settlement was concluded until 1835. The citizens agreed on a line which was established by the legislature as jurisdictional line and each town acquiesced.

William Barlow in 1773 came from Connecticut, built a house near where the old house stood below the road on M. B. Lyon's farm. It is not known what became of him; some say he left during the war, but returned and died in Peru. He was buried on the place in the corner of the Holton lot, where others were buried.

In 1777, Ira Allen, secretary of a convention held at Manchester, wrote in pressing terms to Meshech Weare, president of the provincial council assembled at Exeter, N. H., to send troops or soldiers to Vermont. On the 9th day of July, 1777, President Weare sent a letter to Ira Allen, stating that "They have now determined that a quarter part of the militia of twelve regiments shall be immediately drafted, formed into three battalions under the

EDMUND BATCHELDER.

command of Brigadier General John Stark, and forthwith sent into your
State to oppose the ravages and coming forward of the enemy." It
was furthermore stated that the troops would depend for provisions
upon Vermont. It was also requested that proper persons be sent
to No. 4 (Charlestown), to meet General Stark, and advise with him
relative to the route and disposition of his troops. It is supposed
that General Warner met Stark at No. 4, perhaps others with him.
In a history recently published by C. C. Coffin, it is said General
Stark found a cannon at No 4, which he mounted on cart wheels
and took along with him. It is pictured in Coffin's history, the
horses tugging to take the cannon along, the men lending a hand to
get it over hard places. The route they traveled was through
Springfield, Chester, Andover, Landgrove, Bromley (Peru), corner of
Winhall into Manchester. The troops found a road cut through the
wilderness to Captain Utley's in Landgrove, but here the road
ended. They dined with Captain Utley, and for a part of their
rations he prepared a potash kettle of mush, or in Yankee terms,
hasty pudding. From this place they followed the scarred trees,
removing the impediments in the way or going around them. For
six or eight miles there was no road, and but one opening in the
wilderness, that was on the farm where M. B. Lyon lives, where it
is said a part of the troops camped, the rest going further on and
camping near where Gen. Dudley built his house. He found two
bayonets near the spring, and other indications of a camping place.
Judge Munson, in his History of Manchester, says General Stark
was on the mountain the 6th of August, 1777, and on the 7th came
down to Manchester. This was the largest company of men that
ever traveled through Peru. After this it is probable the delegates
attending the early conventions of the State passed over the
mountain on this route.

EARLY PHYSICAL CONDITION.

Bromley, now Peru, was chartered to be six miles square. It is
bounded on the north by Mount Tabor, on the east by Landgrove,
on the south by Winhall, and on the west by Dorset. It is a
mountain town. The west half of the town is a high mountain
range running north and south through the town, with only one
notch where a road could be made, nearly midway between the
north and south lines of the town. This mountain is the backbone
of the Green Mountains, the water-shed where the water divides.

The Mad Tom rises on the mountain, runs west to East Dorset, where it unites to form the Battenkill river. South of this the Little Mad Tom runs west into the Kill. These waters flow south and west, and empty into the Hudson a little above the monument that marks the spot of Burgoyne's surrender. North of Mad Tom are the head-waters of the Otter Creek, which run west and north to Lake Champlain at Vergennes, thence into the St. Lawrence. The waters on the east side of the mountain flow into the West River, thence southeasterly into the Connecticut and Long Island Sound. The waters of Peru run to the ocean in three different directions. The streams are small but afford good mill privileges for the use of man, and there is not any country on earth that affords cleaner or purer water than flows from the sides of these mountains. Buffom Pond is high on the mountain, containing several acres; it lies in Peru and Mount Tabor, is noted for its good trout fishing. Mud Pond is in the southeasterly part of the town, is a small pond, but is noted for its blood-suckers. The west part of the town is not susceptible of cultivation on account of the steepness and ruggedness of the mountains. The east half was accessible to the early adventurers; it lies pitching to the east and southeast. It was originally covered with a heavy growth of timber, consisting of spruce, hemlock, balsam, pine, white and sugar or rock maple, white and yellow birch, white and black ash, beech, basswood, and some elm. A few lots in the town still have the primitive growth of timber, and are more valuable than much of the cultivated land. The soil is various; in some sections it is a wet, loamy mixture of clay, while other parts are dry and gravely. The land that was covered with hard wood produced bountifully when first cleared, but the more it is cultivated the poorer it becomes. That part covered with dark timber is not as good when first cleared, but cultivation improves it, and is the most desirable for farming purposes, being warmer, more free from stones, and more easily worked than the hard-wood land is.

The first settlers had much to contend with in the early time of the town. With plenty of timber of the best kind, there were no mills to cut it into boards, and it could be used only in its primitive state, hence log houses and barns were the primitive buildings of the first settlers. The first thing for immigrants to do was to select a spot near some spring or rivulet on which they could erect their mansion, then dig a hole in the ground to substitute for a cellar, where through a trap door a ladder was put for stairs, with which to go down for such vegetables as they might have; they were always sure to have a pork barrel well filled, also such fruit as grew natural on the trees. As for a barrel of cider there was no place to get it into the cellar, but that was not the worst of it, there was no cider to put in. Then clear the spot of brush and trees, and cut logs for the dimensions of the house, which was usually one room with a large stone chimney in one end, with a fireplace large enough to hold half a cord of wood. The foundation was laid with logs on the ground, on which the superstructure was erected with logs rolled one upon another, notched at the corners so that the logs would be held in place and lie near together. Cross timbers would be put on for the chamber floor, then the timber for rafters, on which cross ribs were pinned covered with spruce bark or long shingles riven and shaved, which made a roof. The floor was made of split timber, and hewn with an axe, but it was not long before boards could be obtained. The fireplace was large, with a wide stone hearth, the chimney built to the chamber floor with stones, topped out with split sticks laid cob house fashion, well daubed over with clay mortar to make it proof against fire. The cracks between the logs were filled with mortar to keep the cold out and the heat in. A window of six lights on each side gave light in winter and let in air in summer. A doorway was cut out in which was hung a door made of rough boards, nailed together with cleats, and hung on wooden hinges, which, when the door would swing, made music instead of the piano. The door was fastened with a wooden latch with a string on the outside for opening. Pins were driven into the logs on the side and rough boards laid on for the cupboard, which held the china, pewter, tin ware and knives and forks. A large iron crane hung in the fireplace so as to swing backward and forward, furnished with hooks made like the letter S, on which utensils for cooking and washing hung, and made so that they could be swung over the fire or out into the room. The house was then ready to receive the furniture, which was of the simplest kind. For a bedstead, poles were placed on crotches, tables were made with boards or bark laid on poles, while for chairs they used shingle blocks. The real wants or necessities were few and easily supplied. No doubt there was joy and happiness among the early settlers, and the mother never happier than she was when she drew the trundle bed from beneath her own on which to place the little ones, and the little ones happy for such a bed to sleep on under a mother's care. As new emigrants arrived roads were made, the forest melted away, the land was covered with various crops for the sustenance of man and beast, the wild and ferocious animals of the forest were supplanted by domestic ones useful to emigrant settlers. Soon saw mills were erected and trees were made into useful lumber, framed houses and barns began to appear. With all this the wants and necessities of the inhabitants increased, and has continued to do so until the present time.

The first settlers of Peru were limited in means to furnish homes and utensils for necessary use, and their farming tools were of very primitive kind. They had no carts or wagons, and at first sleds of the rudest kind, with stone boats, were in use summer and winter. Hay and grain were taken to barns and stacks on sleds that had no iron about them. The first ploughs were made with one handle, beam framed into it, with a pin in the upper end by which to hold it, wooden mould board covered with strips of iron nailed on, with a point of steel which could be taken off and sharpened. Soon ploughs had two handles. About 1825 cast iron ploughs came into use. There has been a constant improvement in ploughs. The first carts were without iron, except bands around the hubs and boxes in the hub for axletree to roll in. The felloes were six inches wide, doweled at the ends with pins to hold the blocks together, and were called block wheels. With these clumsy wheels, and a cart body equally as clumsy, the work was done. Soon straps of iron were nailed on the felloes for tires. Great improvements have been made in carts. Harrows at first were crotches cut from trees, with about seven iron teeth to scratch among the stumps. Time has improved all these tools. The best are now used, with the mower added. About 1815 the first one-horse wagon was brought into town by Esquire Bigelow, and by 1825 one-horse wagons were in general use. The only spring that they had was in the axletree, the body being bolted to the axletree. Ninety years have made a great change.

The farmers in those days calculated to raise half an acre of flax, selecting the most feasible land. Well prepared by enriching it with the finest of fertilizers, they had well cultivated a good seed bed for flax seed. It grew from two to three feet high, and no crop looked handsomer or more beautiful than the flax patch when in full bloom. It is usually ready for harvest in August. Pulling flax, oh, what a job. All the help indoors and out was called into requisition to pull the flax. When dry it was bound in small bundles and the seed pounded off, which was carefully saved. It was a cash article and found ready sale. The flax was carried to the smooth field, thinly and evenly spread to rot; when properly rotted it was bound in large bundles and stowed away in the roof of some shed or other out place. In February or March, on bright sunny days, the farmer would have his bundles of flax on the fences or wood piles to dry. He and the boys in the barn breaking and swingling. The fibre would be cleaned of shives, becoming soft and pliable and ready for the good matron of the house to take in hand, with all the girls she had to help (it was no disgrace for young ladies to spin and weave in those days). The house was furnished with all the implements for making cloth, such as the hatchel, tow cards, linen wheel, tow wheel and quill wheel. Warping bars and loom were the machinery of this factory. The power to run it was the feet, hands and brain of the old and young women who had skill and the will to manufacture with their own fingers the material for their finest and best garments, and they were their own mantua makers. In the spring you would hear the buzzing of the wheels and the strike of the loom, and see the large bunches of the yarn hung around to grace the kitchen. They would make their own white diaper tablecloths and towels, white underlinen, striped gowns, checked handkerchiefs, aprons, etc., in which clothes they were fitted out for any company in any place. They would manufacture their husbands', fathers' and brothers' white summer shirts, trousers and frocks. It was common to see webs of tow and linen cloth spread on the grass to whiten out by sprinkling water on it, let the sun dry it, and so continue to do until it was white. Tow cloth had a ready market, and quantities were made to sell. Farmers kept sheep for domestic purposes. In June the wool was sorted into bundles according to its quality, sent to the carding machine and made into rolls. The whole paraphernalia of cloth-making machinery was called into requisition for converting the wool into cloth. Beech, hemlock and butternut bark, with sumach berries were in demand for dyeing, and withal the blue dye stood in the corner of the fireplace. The plain woolen cloth was made for bed blankets, and some was sent to the clothier to be colored, fulled and dressed for the best suits, some was colored in the yarn to be woven into striped cloth for frocks; most of the men wore them. Some of the yarn was knit into stockings for family use and to sell, and some knit into leggings shaped to the foot to wear instead of boots in the deep snow.

WILD ANIMALS.

In the first settlement of the town the wild animals were numerous and troublesome. The wolf, bear, deer, moose, lynx and catamount roamed in the forest unmolested. The early settlers invaded their rights, and they showed resentment by taking a pig, a lamb, a sheep or a calf, and would enter the corn field after the green corn. The farmers used means to catch and destroy them, shooting and trapping them. Tame men and wild animals did not live on good terms together. In 1832 the wolves were troublesome, taking animals from the barnyard or anywhere near it. A pack of wolves was heard one night, and in the morning two men concluded to follow them. The snow was deep, with a crust. Isaac G. Long and Seth Lyon put on snowshoes and took all the rations they could carry with their guns. They started in chase after the wolves on the mountain, pursued a northeasterly course into the woods, then north from the Benjamin Barnard's inn, where they made good progress, but night came on before they found the wolves. They camped under a tree without fire or covering. The chase was continued by daylight the next morning, but no wolves were seen, and during the day the snowshoes gave out. Being on the mountain they did not know how far they were from any habitation. The second night came without seeing any wolves, and they camped the same as before. The third morning they concluded that the wolves were safer than they were, for it had turned very cold. They came to a branch of the Otter Creek, which they followed on the bank in the day and by the water at night until they came to Woodman's road, where Mr. Long's strength failed him and he could go no further. Mr. Lyon sat him on a log and followed down the road, which led to Danby Borough, where he obtained help to go back for Mr. Long. They found him helpless, his hands frozen to his gun. His boots had to be cut from his feet, and his limbs were badly frozen. He lost his toes on one foot, and the big toe on the other, and suffered the most excruciating pain for weeks after he got home. It affected his health for life. Mr. Lyon was a younger man, with great muscular strength, and said that if Mr. Long had been able to keep going it would have been all right with them. It was an experience they did not care to have again. One of the wolves that they followed appeared to have a defective foot, and afterwards a wolf was caught in an adjacent town with a foot demoralized. Mr. Long went a journey to get the pelt of the wolf which he followed to his sorrow, and used it to wrap around his feet, as much as to say, I have got the animal and will make use of it for my comfort.

It was said that one moose was captured in the town a little south of Charles Batchelder's house. Moose would live on the bark of moosewood trees. Occasionally a bear makes his appearance, but he is either captured by the shrewd hunter or thinks it is wisdom to part company with mankind. Other wild animals are not very plentiful The hedgehog and porcupine still linger on the mountain range, and will as long as the bark of the birch and beech will furnish food for living.

EARLY SETTLERS.

Many of the early settlers of Peru came from the northeast part of Massachusetts, from the towns of Princeton, Westminster and Gardner, and from the south part of New Hampshire. David Stratton came to town in 1795, and settled on the top of Stratton hill at the fork of the road in the south corner of J. P. Long's pasture. His brother, Richard Stratton, had a house east of David's, in the pasture now owned by Dexter Batchelder. They built a frame barn on the west side of the road in the field owned by Dexter Batchelder. David and Richard Stratton deeded the north cemetery to the town A. D. 1803. Very little is known of them. Their sister was the wife of Aaron Killam. The farm was afterwards owned by Jacob Odel, of Mount Vernon, N. H., who erected the house in which Dexter Batchelder now lives.

Jonathan Butterfield built a house about 1775 on the top of the mountain, north from the house occupied by Dickinson. It was occupied as a public house until the turnpike was built. This was the first tavern in town, and did a good business, cutting large quantities of hay. The buildings were large and commodious. This farm was a pitched lot, settled before the allotment of the town, and the first road that was built over the mountain ran past the house. Aaron Killam was the third settler in town in 1797, owning the farm now occupied by Charles Farnum. His wife was the sister of David Stratton. He had a good farm with good buildings, and a family of boys and girls. He left town with his family in 1823, settling in Oswego County, N. Y.

Reuben Bigelow came to town in 1797, and began on the farm now owned by Merrill G. Walker, building his house and barn on the hill southwest of the present buildings. His barn was the first framed building in town. He came from Princeton, Mass., and moved his family into town the first day of March, 1800, having two children.

CHILDREN OF REUBEN BIGELOW.

Abigail M. Dr. L. G. Whiting, of Chester, died 1888, aged 92 years.

Susan M. Aaron Burton, lived in Chester and Peru, died in Manchester, 1868.

Lucinda M. Cephas Tuthill, lived in Landgrove, moved to Illinois in 1839, now living.

Deborah M. Baker, lived in Brattleboro, he died and she M. Mr. Shearer, moved to Michigan, now living.

Demietta M. Russell Tuthill, lived in Peru until 1837, moved to Illinois, now living.

Miles M. in the West, died there about 1836.

Laura M. Rev. Mr. Fairchilds, living in Wisconsin.

Orrilla M. Mr. Nichols in Virginia, living now.

Caroline M. Mr. Nichols in Virginia, living now.

Orlando M. in the West, died on the way to California.

Dr. Asa M. in Indiana, practiced medicine there, moved to Toledo, Ohio, practiced medicine and was professor in the Medical School at Toledo, died 1889.

The Esquire Bigelow farm, after his decease in 1834, went into the hands of his son-in-law, Aaron Burton. At that time the buildings were the same as they had been for a long time. A large house, on the ground, one story high, with a large and long L. on the west end ending towards the road, stairs with several steps to get into the bar room, which was in the southeast corner of the house; it was a long room with a bar in the northwest corner. This house stood southwest of the present house, with two barns north from the house. A long open shed entered north from the present house used to accommodate the traveling public, with cribs and room for grain in the end. Over the brook, south of the house, was a row of shops for shoe shops, hair shop, paint shop, and on the corner next to Adams's road was a blacksmith shop; these were where the wall now stands. A large barn road over the brook just above the road which was used for storage. Aaron Burton moved or took all these buildings away, and built a cheap house on the same spot as the old one. F. P. Batchelder bought the place of Burton in 1841, and lived on it for

STOWELL BARNARD.

three or four years, then sold it to Nathaniel and S. B. Russell, who lived on the place fifteen years or more, then selling it to Leonard Howard, who sold the place to M. G. Walker about 1869 or '70. Walker built the present house and lived in it several years, then sold it to the present owners and moved to Manchester. Until 1827 this place was the city of the town, being the business centre. All the public meetings were held in the school house. The mechanics' shops, the hotel, the postoffice was here, and the tannery was here run by Frederick Holton.

Benjamin Barnard, senior, came to town from Westminster, Mass., in 1800, and his was the fifth family in town. He began on the farm where Mr. Crossman now lives, building a log house in the orchard east of the present house. He had a family of four boys and four girls, was a soldier of the revolution, and received a wound in his leg which made him a cripple for life, for which he drew a pension. It was with difficulty that he could get around to work on his farm, so the latter part of his life he spent at shoemaking. He and his wife (whose maiden name was Lucy Wood) were persons of great energy and perseverance, being two of the eight who organized the Congregational church, always making themselves useful in its interests. They also made themselves very useful to the sick and afflicted, Mrs. Barnard being frequently called instead of a doctor to prescribe for and nurse the sick. They trained their children in the way they should walk to be useful citizens and to sustain the insitutions of the gospel, which extended down to their grandchildren. They remained on the old homestead until death removed them. Benjamin Barnard, senior, died 1837, aged 87 years; Lucy, his wife, died 1849, aged 97 years.

CHILDREN OF BENJAMIN BARNARD.

Louisa M. Leonard Weed, moved to Oswego County, N. Y.

Josiah M. Hannah Byam, lived in Peru until 1834, then moved to Oberlin, Ohio, where he lived and died, aged 93 years.

Lucy M. Gen. Peter Dudley, always lived in Peru, died in 1840.

Hannah M. Jonathan Dudley of Andover, lived there until 1837, when they moved to Pittsfield, Ohio, and lived to a ripe old age. Their children are prominent citizens of Lorain County.

Benjamin M Hepsibeth Phillrick, lived in Peru.

Stowell M. Mary Burton of Chester, lived in Peru.

Joseph M. Lucinda Bennett of Peru, where he lived a few years and then emigrated to Virginia. where, by second marriage, he became a slave-holder, and during the rebellion he was unjustly imprisoned over a difficulty about slavery; he died in 1864.

Nancy M. Deacon John Batchelder of Peru, died in Peru 1882, aged 92 years.

Deacon Thomas Wyman came into town in February, 1801, with his wife and five children, being the sixth family in town. He settled on the Deacon Wyman farm, building his log house west of the orchard and north of the brickyard, on the first road that ran through the town. His house was built previous to moving his family. For a place to shelter his oxen, which had drawn him and his family from Princeton, Mass., he shoveled four feet of snow from a spot large enough for them and a cow to stand on, set in posts with crotches, on which he laid poles covered with hemlock boughs, this being a substitute for a barn. He had to draw hay from Landgrove to feed his cattle. Deacon Wyman cut the first tree on his farm for clearing, and he soon had a productive farm, keeping a large stock. He built a good set of buildings on the road west of the present buildings on the farm. He manufactured brick for twenty years or more, commencing in 1808.

CHILDREN OF DEACON THOMAS WYMAN.

Warren, the eldest, went to Black River country in New York, and died there. His daughter, Harriet, lived with her grandparents, who brought her up in Peru.

Parker M. Lydia Byard, lived in Peru some years. He was gate keeper for the turnpike company several years, then moved to Manchester, where he died in 1882, aged 90 years. His wife died some years before.

Sally, only daughter, M. Levi Pease of Weston, moved to western New York and died there.

Oliver M. Susan Kimball of Windham, for his first wife.

Dana M. Annis Adams, lived in Peru, Annis died September 4, 1865, aged 63 years. He married the second wife, who now lives in Peru. Dana died in 1882, aged 83 years.

Thomas was the first child born in Peru, he M. Louisa Persons of Weston, who died in 1858, aged 54 years. Thomas always lived in Peru, and died February 13, 1880, aged 78 years and 4 months.

Jonathan Russell M. Sally A. Moody, lived in Peru for a short time, then moved over the mountain; he died at his son's home in the northern part of York State.

Levi S. M. Mary Ann Godfrey, lived in Landgrove; he died suddenly in 1854, aged 43 years.

Washington M. Caroline Jamison of Manchester; he is now living.

Russell, Levi and Washington drove the stage from Chester to Manchester until it was taken off the road. They were safe and prudent drivers.

CHILDREN OF OLIVER AND SUSAN WYMAN.

Kimball M., lives in Bennington.

Sarah M.

Lucretia M., lives in Manchester.

CHILDREN OF OLIVER AND SALLY WYMAN.

Joel, Lucinda and Myron.

Oliver Wyman built the first house and barn where Albert Simonds lives now, and owned the stone mill for a time, also the farm where Mrs. Leonard lives. In 1854 he moved to York State, then to Illinois, where he died in 1878, aged 85 years.

Deacon Seth Lyon came to Peru from Princeton, Mass., about 1803, and built a log house on the hill in Whitney's lot on the old road; he also built a frame barn, which is the south barn of M. B. Lyon. He lived on this place some years, then began on the Lyon farm, which is south of the Hapgood place. He cleared this farm and built the house and barn, living there until he died in 1844, aged 83 years.

CHILDREN OF DEACON SETH LYON.

Freeman M. Louisa Pease of Weston, lived in Peru and Landgrove, died October 21, 1866, aged 77 years. His first wife died February 25, 1828, aged 38 years. His second wife was Susan Towns of Andover.

Dorcas M. William Green, lived in Peru; they moved to Ohio twice, died there.

Sophia M. Asa Simonds, lived in Peru, died in 1869.

Seth M. Hepsibath Jones of Derry; they had four children when she died. He then married Samantha Ballard, who had three children. He moved to Jamaica about 1836, living there until he died.

Lydia M. Goodell Walker, lived in Peru, died in 1884.

Patty M. D. Temple of Stratton, died there.

Joel M. Jane Batchelder, lived in Peru, died in 1870.

CHILDREN OF JOEL LYON.

Dexter, unmarried, lives in Peru.

Marcellus died while a young man in Peru.

Nancy, unmarried, lives in Peru.

Mark B. m. Abbie M. Rideout of Dorset, lives in Peru.

CHILDREN OF FREEMAN LYON.

Freeman m. S. Smith of New York, lives in Peru.

Rhoda m. Chapin.

Lydia m. Franklin Sheldon, lives in Winhall.

Simeon m. Mabel Chandler, lived in Peru, moved to Shushan, N. Y., died there.

Charles m. Susan A. (Burton) Hatch, lives in Shushan, N. Y.

Minerva m. A. Cleveland, lived in Shushan, N. Y.; she died in 1887.

Asa went West.

CHILDREN OF SETH AND HEPSIBATH LYON.

Stanley m. Miss Barnard of Winhall, lives in Derry.

Hepsibath m. Albert Bennett of Peru, went West.

Harriet M., lives in New York State.

Sophia M., lives in New York State.

CHILDREN OF SETH AND SAMANTHA LYON.

Daniel m. Miss Sage, lives in New York city.

One daughter m. Cushman, lives in New York city.

Stowell Barnard came to town with his parents in 1800, when about 12 or 13 years of age. He had what education could be obtained at the common school of the town, which was somewhat limited in time and capacity to teach. Stowell was a large, muscular man, able to cope with any man in doing a day's work. He had good judgment, was ever ready and willing to do his share in supporting the institutions of the town, whether political, educational or religious, but never sought office of any kind, or cared for it. He was one of the best farmers in town and had one of the best farms. He made more butter and cheese than any other farmer in town. He married Mary Burton of Chester, living on his father's farm and taking care of his parents. His mother died at the age of 97 years. He died at the age of 72 years in 1864, with a cancer inwardly.

CHILDREN OF STOWELL BARNARD.

Avaline m. George Whitney, lived at Glens Falls, N. Y., died in 1850.

Eleanor m. Edwin Gilson, lives in Chester.

Lydia m. Samuel Kelley, lives in Greenfield.

Abigal m. F. P. Batchelder, lives in St. Louis, Mo.

PETER DUDLEY, JUN.

Lucy M. Henry Haynes, lives in Granville, Ill.

Benjamin S. M. Fanny Davis, lives in Dakota.

Emma M. Croydon Dutton, died in Windham, 1885.

Burton M., lives in St. Louis, Mo.

H. O. Davis came from Manchester to Peru in 1833, and bought the farm on which Charles Farnum now resides, of Seth Lyon, Junior. He was a hatter by trade, and manufactured hats for several years. His goods had a good reputation in the community. The young men who wanted a dandy hat would go to Davis's in Manchester to get a white fur stove-pipe hat before he came to Peru. Hence he had a ready sale for his goods. In order to make hats he neglected the farm, which, although a good one, needed to be worked. Mr. Davis and family were good members of society, his wife being a niece of Judge Keyes of Brattleboro. He died in 1889, aged 82 years.

CHILDREN OF H. O. DAVIS.

Abbie M. Charles Batchelder, lives in Peru.

George K. M., has lived in New York city, now in Peru.

Fox M., lives in Manchester, N. H.

Frances M. Mr. Savage, lived in Manchester, N. H., both dead. Buried at Peru.

Jared M. Miss Amsden, lives in Lee, Mass.

Russell Lamb was a member of Mr. Davis's family at the time they came to Peru, and lived with them until he became of age. He married and settled in Wells, Vt., where he has prospered.

Moses Killam began on the place where Alfred Williams now resides. He died young, leaving a widow, who lived in town for a short time, then went to Ohio and married a man by the name of Barker. Their only child, Maria, married Jonathan Walker of Peru.

Silas Holt began on the Morse place in 1802. His wife died soon after and was buried in a lot in the southwest corner of the Holton farm. Soon after her death he sold the place to Amos Morse and left town. This farm is west of Almon Adams's. Mr. Morse moved out of town and Stephen Bennett lived on the place for a while. Zimri Whitney was the last man that lived on it.

Joel Adams came into the town in 1804 from Princeton, Mass., and built a log house on the farm now owned by Almon Adams. He built all the buildings on the farm. Mr. Adams was a professional teamster, teaming to Boston and Troy for many years, and until the railroads made it unnecessary. In 1840 he left his place on the hill to his son Abel and bought the Deacon Wyman farm, where he lived until his death in 1862, being 82 years old. His wife's maiden name was Mary Tenney; she died March 28, 1872, aged 95 years.

CHILDREN OF JOEL ADAMS.

Annis M. Dana Wyman, lived in Peru, died August, 1865.

Joel M. Abigal Batchelder of Peru. He was born in Peru and always lived there. He was a man of good habits, as well as a useful citizen. He was a drummer in the militia company and led the singing in the Congregational church for a long time, being a useful member. He died suddenly of paralysis in 1864, aged 59 years; his wife died in 1881.

Abel M. Damarius Gibson of Londonderry. He was a fifer in the militia company and an active member of the Methodist church. In 1849 he moved to South Derry, where he died in 1855. His widow is still living.

CHILDREN OF JOEL ADAMS, JR.

Everett M. A. Aldrich, lives in Peru.

Celina M. Mason Sage, died in Wardsboro in 1878.

CHILDREN OF ABEL ADAMS.

Warren, Charles, Elvira, George, Jerome, Helen and Abbie, all born in Peru.

The house on the Holton place was built early, but the builder is not known. James Grant taught several terms of school in the house previous to 1808. When David Sawyer moved into the house he carried on a tannery business for some years, selling the place and business to Timothy Maynard, who continued the business until 1819. He sold out to Frederick Holton of Westminster, who moved into the house in the autumn of 1819. Mr. Holton was a man full of jokes and fun, and an excellent tanner, his leather being in high repute in all the adjoining towns. He died of consumption in 1848, and his widow died at her daughter Harriet's house in Illinois in 1866.

CHILDREN OF MR. HOLTON.

Sophia M. William Weymouth of Westminster, moved to Peru in 1858, and lived on the Holton place. He was the first man to enlist in the army from Peru; he enlisted on October 10, 1861, and went to join the Army of the Potomac, where he died. His body was sent to Peru and buried, it being just two months from the day he left home. Sophia, his wife, died in Peru August 26, 1878, aged 61 years.

Louise M. Moses Elliot, went to Pittsfield, Ohio, then to Granville, Ill., where she now resides, having two boys.

Harriet M. Charles E. Barnard, in 1865, moved to Granville, Ill. Had a family of four sons and four daughters.

Orrilla died in Peru in 1856.

1144516

Angeline died in Peru of consumption May 2, 1862, aged 33 years.

David Wyman, brother of Deacon Thomas Wyman, began on the lot east of the Holton farm, building a log house and framed barn, but stayed only a few years. He sold the place to Benjamin Ballard and moved to Manchester.

Deacon Benjamin Ballard moved into town in 1814, built the house in which Whittemore Thomas lived, on the David Wyman lot. He also moved the David Wyman barn to his house, then sold the place to Mark Batchelder and went to live on the Burt farm for a while, moving to Manchester in 1845 with his son Benjamin.

CHILDREN OF DEACON BENJAMIN BALLARD.

Sally went to Manchester and died of a cancer.

Samantha M. Seth Lyon, lived in Peru, moved to Jamaica, died in 1881 of a cancer.

Horace studied medicine and graduated at Castleton Medical College, settled in Williamstown, Mass., died in 1833.

Benjamin S. M. Betsey Warren, commenced on the place east of the Goodell Walker farm, built the house now on the place, then sold it and bought the Simonds mill. He repaired the mill and put in a large breast wheel, and built the Ira Walker house. He sold out to Edward Batchelder and moved to Manchester in 1845, left there and went to Cleveland, Ohio, then to Long Island, where he buried his wife, after which he went to Kansas for a time, then came back and settled down in South Orange, N. J., where he died in May, 1889, aged 79 years.

Josiah Hapgood was born in Marlboro, Mass., 1779, and came to Peru in 1800. He began on new land near O. P. Simonds's homestead, but disposed of the place and bought a wild lot where the Josiah Hapgood buildings are. Mr. Hapgood grappled with the forest single-handed, working on his land during the summer and returning to Marlboro to spend the winter. In 1805 he contracted for a barn 30 x 40 feet, to be built for $40; the same barn is now on the place. In the season of 1806 he married Elizabeth Maynard of Marlboro and moved to Peru, living in the new barn for a time. They did their cooking by the side of a large rock which is to be seen to this day near the barn. He soon built a house and settled down. His son Jonathan inherited the paternal acres, got married, and built a new house on the site of the old one, which was moved to be used as an out-building. Mr. Hapgood and his wife were kind and obliging neighbors and useful citizens of the town, good members of the church and always ready to sustain it by their presence and means. Widow Lovina Maynard, Mrs. Hapgood's mother, came to live with the family in 1813, where she died in 1841. Mrs. Maynard had a Bible of her mother's, in which the following was written: "Lovina Barns's Bible. Presented by her honored father as a bridal gift, with charge to read and study it daily with care and delight, praying that it may make her wise unto salvation through faith in Jesus Christ," which charge she kept while living. The date of her marriage is 1776. Mr. Hapgood and his wife endured many hardships and privations incident to new settlements, but they were always willing to share what they did have with their neighbors. On one occasion, at a funeral, the mourners being minus shoes, Mrs. Hapgood lent them all she had, leaving herself without any. For a substitute, she took her husband's logging trousers and cut enough cloth out of them to make shoes to wear to the funeral. She walked most of the way barefooted to save them for the end of the journey. When she arrived home she placed the cloth of the shoes back on the trousers, so as to be ready for the farmer's use again. Mr. Hapgood was a plain man, but everything he had was good. He was always satisfied with his lot, therefore always happy, and his wife was just the same. He died in 1857, aged 78 years; his wife died in 1853.

CHILDREN OF JOSIAH HAPGOOD.

Joseph Jackson M. Hepsibah Barnard, lived in Peru.

Elizabeth M. Jesse Brown, died in Peru in 1837.

Lovina M. Alvah Brooks of Halifax, died in Illinois in 1869.

Persis M. William Whitney, lived in Peru, died February 16, 1877, aged 65 years.

Mary M. John Q. Adams of Peru, died in 1880, aged 66 years.

Jonathan M. Aurelia (Davis) Marsh of Reading, Vt., lived on the homestead in Peru; his wife had been married before and had one son, Dr. James Marsh of Factory Point, with whom they both died, Aurelia in 1882, and Jonathan in 1883. Both were buried at Peru. They were useful citizens.

Almira M. Barton Aldrich of Westmoreland, N. H.

Ruth M. Carlos Davis of Reading, where they now reside.

Joseph M. Mary Gates of Stowe, Mass., lived there, died in 1887.

Cyrus Staples began on a wild lot on the farm east of the Joel Lyon farm in 1802. He married Orpha Whitney and had a large family, namely, Eunice, Sally, Edith, Silas, Tryphena, Tryphosa, Hannah, Samuel, Mary, Emily and Sarah. Silas was the only one that settled in Peru. He married Mary Reynolds of Derry and lived on the Fosgot farm until 1855, when he moved to Pennsylvania. All the other children settled down in the West. Mr. Staples buried his wife about 1837, then married again and left town. He instituted the only Baptist church in town.

David Robbins came to his farm about 1823, on which was a log house that had been built by Mason Tarbell. Mr. Robbins was a hard working man. He raised a large family, and died April 3, 1872, aged 84 years. The widow and two sons, Samuel and Alvin, live on the farm.

David Davis began on land north of Mr. Robbins, built a small house, laid the foundation and built a dam, then put up a frame for a saw mill, but never finished it. He was found dead, hung by the neck, in his own house, in March, 1853, aged 58 years.

Scammel Burt came into the town early. He married Sally Parker of Chester, and lived in a house east of David Simonds, known as the Densmore place. He was burnt out about 1825. By the help of the townspeople, who were the only insurance in town, he built a house near the Stowell Barnard place at the foot of the hill, on the road. He was a hard-working, industrious man, full of jokes and fun, and a kind and useful citizen. He had a large family, and when they were all of age he went to live with his son Parker on the Atkins place, where he died in 1857. His wife died in 1877, aged 92 years.

CHILDREN OF SCAMMEL BURT.

Joseph Parker, unmarried, had fits for forty years, died in town in 1879.

Adaline M. Cyrus Bailey of Andover, died young

Rhodolphus M. in Michigan, died there in 1879.

Gracie M. Wm. C. Strong, who went to the war, and while he was there two of their sons died at her mother's of diphtheria.

Joshua M. Rebecca Bennett, owned and lived on the Killam farm, erecting all the buildings now on the farm, but sold out in

1865 and moved to Michigan with his family. He died there.

Sally M. Cyrus Bailey of Andover, lived and died there.

Mary Ann died in childhood.

Justin M., settled in Andover, now lives in Peru and owns the farm his brother Parker had. He has two daughters.

Ezra M., lives in Mendon, Vt.

Justin is the only one of the family remaining in Peru.

Isaac Hill married Miss Adams, a sister of Hannah Adams, who wrote a history of the Jews and a history of New England. Mr. Hill's family were talented. His son Thomas studied law with Gov. Skinner and settled in Bangor, Maine, becoming eminent in his profession, and Moses studied law and practiced in Ohio. Isaac Hill began new on the farm where Justin Burt lives. He lived there some years and then returned to Massachusetts, selling the farm to Mr. Atkins, who lived on it a number of years. General Peter Dudley owned it after Mr. Atkins, when Francis Bennett, Benjamin Ballard and some other families lived on it as his tenants. General Peter Dudley sold the place to Joseph P. Burt in 1837, in whose name it has remained ever since.

William Pollard began new on the farm where John Byard lives, which is known as the Pollard farm. Mr Pollard was the first town clerk east of the mountain. He died early of consumption, leaving a widow, a daughter and son. The daughter married David Gleason, living below the gate on the turnpike road. Kittredge Parker owned and lived on this place from 1837 to 1843, when he sold it to Francis Bennett, who sold it to Lewis White. Mr. White built the house on it and sold out to Asa and Calvin Phillips, who lived on it and improved the buildings and farm very much. Asa Phillips died on this place. Merrill G. Walker bought the farm of Calvin Phillips, and Harlan Batchelder bought it from him, living on it two or three years. It was then sold to Martin Granger, who stayed on it a short time and then sold it to James Lakin. He occupied it only a few years, selling it to John Byard, the present occupant.

The farm on which J. G. Walker lives was called the Fosgot place. Mendal Fosgot began new on this farm and built the first buildings, but did not stay on it long. Several families have lived there. George W. Whitcomb lived on this farm, then Mr. Phillips for a short time, after which Nahum Benjamin owned it several years. He sold it to Thomas Wyman and J. J. Hapgood in 1835 and joined the Mormans, going, with his family, to live with them in

Ohio. It is supposed that they afterwards went with them to Nauvoo, Ill., and then probably went to Salt Lake. They were the only family that apostatized to that sect from Peru. Silas Staples bought the farm of Deacon Wyman and J. J. Hapgood, improving the farm and buildings very much. He married Mary Reynolds of Derry. They had two children, Merrill and Emeline, who went with them to Pennsylvania in 1856, where they now reside. Nathaniel and O. N. Russell bought the place of Silas Staples. They stayed on it several years, built new barns and improved the farm, then sold it to J. G. Batchelder, who resided on the farm until 1870. He sold the place to B. L. Barnard, who kept it one year and then sold out to J. G. Walker, who is the present occupant. He has improved the place very much.

Moses Adams came to town about 1823. He began new on the lot south of the farm Mr. Byard lived on, and built the buildings on the farm. His wife died in 1850, aged 58 years. He then went to live in Reading, Vt., and married again in West Windsor.

CHILDREN OF MOSES ADAMS.

Moses M. Miss Gale of Windham. He was a Methodist minister and has been on the circuit. He has been a useful man, although his early education was quite limited.

Elias M., died at Winhall in 1852.

Eli M., lives in New York State.

John Q. M. Mary Hapgood of Peru, and always lived there. His wife died in 1880; he then married Widow Mary (Lincoln) Bennett.

Louisa M. Nathaniel Gates, lived in Chester.

Laura M. Sewell Covey, lived in Weston. Laura is dead. Mr. Covey was a soldier in the rebellion, and after his return went West.

CHILDREN OF JOHN Q. ADAMS.

Almon M., lives in Peru.

Alma M., lives in Iowa.

Carrie M., lives in Jamaica, Vt.

Aaron Byard and his wife, Anna Dunster, came to Peru in 1802. They began on the farm south of Stowell Barnard's, it being a lease lot. He built the buildings and improved the farm, but sold it in 1823 to Mr. Elliot, and bought the Maynard place. He put up a frame for a house, shingled it, and moved into it before the sides were boarded up, hanging the bed clothes on the sides, but he soon had comfortable buildings. Mr. Byard was a natural farmer, a great observer of nature's laws. He was the best veterinary surgeon that ever lived in town. No one could care for flocks and herds better than Uncle Aaron, or could swing a scythe to cut a better swath. His health was always delicate, but with prudence and care he lived an active life far beyond his neighbors and townsmen who were stronger and more vigorous. He seldom employed a physician, but studied his own difficulties, finding remedies for the ailments of humanity in the vegetable kingdom around him, and trusted more to the recuperative powers of nature to restore than to the drugs of doctors. Mrs. Byard died in 1871, aged 95 years and 4 months, and Mr. Byard on November 22, 1873, aged 95 years and 5 months.

CHILDREN OF AARON BYARD.

Rexa M. Reuben Tarbell, lived in Rindge, N. H.

Polly M. Mason Tarble, had three children. Mason died at the Brattleboro Asylum, and Polly died at Peru; she was buried on Poplar hill, east of the mill.

Lydia M. Parker Wyman, lived in Peru and Manchester, died in Manchester in 1883.

Anna M. Jonas Bennett, lived and died in Manchester.

Hepsibah M. Charles Childs, lives in Ohio.

Dorcas M. James Pierce, lived and died in Bennington.

Lucy M. John W. Farnum, lived in Peru, died in 1867, aged 52.

Maria M. Dexter French, lived in Manchester, died in 1889.

Aaron T. M. Jane McMullin, lived in Peru, moved to Townshend.

CHILDREN OF LUCY AND JOHN FARNUM.

David M. Frances Burton, lives in Virginia.

Aaron was killed instantly by the bursting of a mill stone at Arlington, Vt.; aged 23 years.

Mariam M. Edwin B. Simonds, lives in Virginia.

Edwin M. Nellie Smith, lives in Washington, D. C.

Henry M. Betsey Benedict, lives in Arlington.

Lycena M. Eunice Hartwell, lives in Arlington.

Amanda M. Frank Rand, lives in Townshend.

Fred M. Miss Bebee, lives in East Dorset.

CHILDREN OF AARON T. BYARD.

Andrew M. Laura Butler, lives in Chesterfield, N. H.

Fanny M. John D. Miller, lives in Williamsburg, Mass.

John M. Anna Simonds, lives in Townshend. He was a farmer and fox hunter.

MRS. CHARLES LYON.

CHARLES LYON.

Stella M. Hiram Reynolds, itinerant preacher.

Jennie M. John Howard, of Jamaica.

Willard lives in New York city.

Jonathan Elliot came into town about 1822 and bought the Byard farm, but lived on it only a short time, selling it to Obel Adams. He then bought the Asa Simonds farm and built a new house on it. Mr. Elliot sold out to G. Walker and moved to Ohio with his family. Their names were Asa, Levi, Oliver, Moses, Francis, Jonathan, Jason and Clarissa, most of whom settled in Ohio. Moses lives in Granville, Ill. John Emerson bought this farm of Obel Adams, his brother living on it for some years. Mr. Emerson sold to Cephas Bailey, who moved on to the place about 1844. Mr. Bailey married Caroline Wright. Their children's names were Romanzo, Harrison, Victoria, Joseph and Nancy. In 1856 Mr. Bailey sold his farm to A. P. D. Simonds, and moved to Pennsylvania with his family. This was the farm where Mr. Simonds was killed. Clark Bryant also lived on this place several years.

Benjamin Williams began new on the farm where Calvin Phillips lives, clearing the land and erecting the buildings. He sold the farm to Calvin Phillips in 1868, and bought F. P. Batchelder's farm, where he died on October 29, 1872, aged 74 years. His wife died in 1888.

CHILDREN OF BENJAMIN WILLIAMS.

Lewis M. Tryphena Phelps of Grafton, lives in Winhall.

George M. Lucy Gale of Winhall, died in Jamaica.

Mariah M. Samuel Phelps, lives in Grafton.

Alfred M. Maria Penfield, lives in Peru.

Calvin M. Widow Angeline (Eddy) Simonds, lives in Peru.

Asa Phillips came to Peru about 1835 from New Hampshire. He commenced new on the place south of the Fosgot farm, built a log house and barn, cleared the land of its original growth of timber and made fruitful fields. He then sold the place to Joseph H Simonds and bought the Pollard farm, which he greatly improved. Mr. Phillips was a good farmer. He died on the farm in 1857, aged 57 years, and was the first one that was buried in the new cemetery at the village.

CHILDREN OF ASA PHILLIPS.

Aurilla M. Eliab Stone, went to Michigan.

Asa M. Cyntha Bryant, went to Massachusetts, died there.

Huldah M. Mr. Crouch of Chesterfield, N. H., lived there.

Calvin M. Miss Penfield, lives in Peru on the Williams farm, which he has much improved. He is a first class farmer.

John O. Adams began on the lot west of Calvin Phillips's farm. He cleared it up, built a house and barn, and then sold it to George Williams, who lived on it several years, and then sold out to Calvin Williams, the present owner.

The farm on which Albert Simonds lives was begun by Oliver Wyman, who built the first house and barn on the place. He sold to Mark Batchelder about 1835. He had a blacksmith shop and worked at the business. In 1841 Rufus Bennett bought the place from Mr. Batchelder, who sold it to Lewis White, he selling it to G. S. Hobart, who carried on the place for some years and then sold out to J. H. Simonds and moved to 'Derry. Mr. Simonds built a new barn and house, and bought a new addition to the farm. He died on the farm in 1876, aged 58 years. His son, Albert, married Lina Mills, and is the present owner.

Moses Killam began on the farm where Alfred Williams lives. He built the first buildings on the place. Mr. Killam died here, leaving a son and daughter. The daughter, Maria, married Jonathan Walker, and lived in Landgrove. Mr. J. Bruce lived and died on this place. Lydia Killam also owned it for some time. Asa Simonds then owned it and sold out to Francis Bennett, he selling the place to F. P. Batchelder, who built the present house, made additions to the barns, and improved the farm in every way. In 1862 he sold the place to Stephen Simonds, who sold it to F. P. Batchelder in 1864. He occupied the place until 1869, when he sold out to Benjamin Williams, who died on the farm. His son, Alfred, now lives on it with his mother.

John Chandler built a small house near the saw-mill, where Ira R. Walker lives, but sold it to B. S. Ballard, who built the present house about 1841. He sold the place to George Batchelder, Edward Batchelder buying it from George, who sold it to D. H. Marden; he built a barn and sold out to Ira R. Walker, who is the present owner.

Edward Batchelder sold the saw-mill to Gustavus Albee, who built the house where Calvin Williams now lives, and then sold out to Elijah Simonds, who died, leaving the premises to his family. His family are the present owners. Widow Elijah Simonds married C. Williams, who now occupies the place.

Dana Wyman began on the lot east of Josiah Barnard's farm, built the buildings and lived there a long time. He sold the place

o Zimri Whitney, who sold out to G. K. Davis, and it is now owned
by some of the family. H. O. Davis lived on it a long time.

Josiah Barnard cut the first tree on the farm north of the
Dudley place about 1801. He cleared the land, built the wall and
he buildings. In 1834 he sold out to Stephen Dudley and moved
o Ohio with his family, whose names were: Wood, John, Hannah,
Joseph, Alonzo and Eliza, who all settled near Oberlin, Ohio.
Alonzo studied at Oberlin, becoming a missionary among the Indians
of the Red River country, in the northern part of Minnesota. Josiah
Barnard was an upright man and a useful citizen. He held many of
he important offices of the town, and represented the town of Peru
n a constitutional convention. He lived to be 90 years of age.
Josiah Barnard sold his farm to Stephen Dudley for $800, with all
he improvements on it, in 1834. Mr. Dudley carried on the farm
or two years, and then sold it to John Jackson, who lived on the
place two years. In 1839 Moses and Jessie Rider came from
Grafton and bought the farm of Mr. Jackson. They carried it on
until they both died, when their son, Jesse, came into possession, and
ived on it several years. He sold the place to G. K. Davis.

CHILDREN OF MOSES RIDER.

Jesse M. Mary Dudley, lived in Peru, moved to 'Derry; both died
here.

Harriet M. Solomon Davis, lived in 'Derry.

Mary M. Mr. Fairbanks for her first husband, and Deacon
Edmund Batchelder for the second; lives in Peru.

Carrie M. Daniel Davis, lives in Chester.

CHILDREN OF JESSE RIDER.

Leray M. a lady from the West. He was killed by his engine
falling on him while sawing wood at Bellows Falls.

Helen M. Henry Stiles, lives in Masonville, Iowa.

Caroline M. E. Garfield, lives in Derry.

Guilford, unmarried, lives in Derry.

Julia M., lives in Massachusetts.

G. K. Davis bought the farm of Jesse Rider, and occupied it
several years. He improved the house and then sold it to Theodore
Rand, who carried it on some years, selling out to H. C. Plympton.
Charles G. Hunt, of 'Derry, bought the farm of Mr. Plympton, and is
he present occupant.

The place now owned by G. N. Wyman was commenced by
Benjamin S. Ballard, who built the buildings about 1835, and lived

on the place until 1840. He sold out to Asa Simonds, who occupied
it until his death in 1861. R. F. Manley lived on this farm for a
short time, then Ira R. Walker owned and occupied it until G. N.
Wyman bought it. He is the present owner.

Elijah Simonds and his family came to Peru in 1802 from
Gardner, Mass. He began new on the lot south of the Dudley
farm, building a log house on the old road. He afterwards erected
his frame buildings on the present road, east from the present
buildings and on the opposite side of the road. His house was
clapboarded on the studding with clapboards split and shaved,
it being occupied many years with only that covering on the wall.
Mr. Simonds lived to be quite aged.

CHILDREN OF ELIJAH SIMONDS.

Jonathan went to Richmond.

Elijah went to Massachusetts.

Ezekiel, teacher of music, went to New Orleans.

David m. Anna Byam, lived and died in Peru.

Asa m. Sophia Lyon, lived in Peru.

Lucy m. Mr. Gray, lived in Dorset, moved to Illinois.

Abigal, unmarried, a school teacher, died in New York.

Asa Simonds, son of Elijah Simonds, came to Peru in 1803 with
his parents, from Gardner, Mass. He married Sophia Lyon, and
had a large family. He was elected captain of the militia company
and was deacon in the Congregational church for a time. He built
the mill in 1825 near I. R. Walker's house, which was used for a saw
and grist mill. He came into possession of his father's farm and
had the care of his parents in their decline, but sold the farm to
Jonathan Elliot and bought the place on which A. Williams lives,
near the mill. He sold the mill and farm about 1839 or '40 and
lived on the place that B. S. Ballard occupied. He lived for two
years in Manchester to educate his daughters. His last business
was teaming. He was killed by a falling shed, under which he had
driven to escape a violent gale. He was taken into the Manchester
depot and died on the third day, aged 71 years. His wife died in
1870.

CHILDREN OF ASA SIMONDS.

Sophia m. Edmund Batchelder, lived in Peru; she died in 1856,
aged 41 years.

Mary m. Rev. A. F. Clark, who preached for 12 years in Peru,
now living in Brattleboro.

Abigal M. Isaac Barrows of Dorset, died in November, 1844.

Martha M. C. L. Howe, lives in Brattleboro. Mrs. Howe is
e mother of Mary Howe, the great New England singer.

Dorcas, unmarried. She was a school teacher for more than 30
ars, and gave the Congregational church of Peru $500, the interest
be used for supporting preaching.

A. P. Dodridge M. Fanny Batchelder, lived in Peru. While he
is driving a mowing machine he stepped between the horses, but
st control of them, they dragging the mower over him. He was
·ribly mangled and died in a day or two. He was a good singer,
iding the church choir for some years. His death was in 1865.

William Burkitt M. Alfa Cone, lives in Peru.

Ellen M. A. Gilbert Dexter, editor and proprietor of the Cam-
idge Chronicle, Mass., but now in business in California.

Oscar M. Victoria Bailey, lives in Pennsylvania.

Edward, unmarried, a merchant, lived in Massachusetts, now in
inneapolis.

Goodell Walker came to town in 1817, and married Lydia Lyon.
e built on the Russell farm, but sold it to Ira Russell and bought
e Simonds place of Mr. Elliot, where he lived until he died. He
d a large farm, and improved it and the buildings very much. He
·eded the place to his son, Porter J., who occupied it a few years
id then sold it to J. G. Walker, the present owner. Goodell died
1875, aged about 79 years.

CHILDREN OF GOODELL WALKER.

John G. M. Hannah Davis, lived in Peru, now in 'Derry.

Ira R. M. Catharine Wyman, lives in Peru.

Seth L. M. Abbie Drury, lives on the Dudley farm in Peru.

Jerusha M. Joshua Barnard, lives in Winhall.

Eunice M. Isaac Barnard, died in Jamaica.

Merrill G. M. Rosetta Stiles, lived on the Bigelow farm in Peru,
w in Manchester.

Duane M. Irene Stoddard, died in Peru in 1863, aged 30 years.

Porter J. M. Lucy Dudley; she died in 1865, aged 29 years. He
en married Martha Gilligan, lived in Manchester, now in Chicago.

Janette M. O. N. Russell, died in Peru in 1863, aged 22 years.

Mary Jane M. Josiah H. Whitney, lives on the B. Barnard farm
Peru.

Benjamin Barnard, jr., commenced on the farm now occupied
· Josiah H. Whitney. In 1804 he built a log house and barn

north from the present buildings, in the pasture on the old road; the nursery of apple trees marks the spot. In 1813 he built where the present buildings are, but the house has been replaced by one built by his son Charles, and occupied by B. Barnard and his wife until his death in 1864. Charles E., his son, had the homestead, which he sold in 1865 to M. G. Walker, who sold it to Josiah H. Whitney, who lives there at the present time.

CHILDREN OF BENJAMIN BARNARD, JR.

Hepsibath M. J. J. Hapgood, lives in Peru.

Elizabeth M. Israel Haynes, lives in Wilmington.

Nancy M. Ira K. Batchelder, lived in Peru until 1869, then went to Townshend.

Emily M. Ruel Gibson of Derry, died in Alstead, N. H., in 1879

Luke B. M. Aramintha Haynes of Wilmington, lives in Wilmington.

Charles E. M. Harriet Holton of Peru, lived in Peru until 1865 then moved to Granville, Ill., living there at the present time.

Seth B. M. Mary Fox of Wilmington, living there until his death in 1885.

The farm west of Benjamin Barnard's place was begun early by Mr. Graves, who was a useful citizen. In 1817 he sold the farm to Thomas Sumner, he selling it to Reuben Walker, who came from Jamaica. He lived on this place and in a small house that was built for him on the turnpike road near the Jesse Brown road, and died at his son's in Landgrove.

CHILDREN OF REUBEN WALKER.

Goodell M. Lydia Lyon, always lived in Peru.

Sally M. Ira Russell, lived and died in Peru.

Jonathan M. Maria Killam, died in Landgrove.

Reuben went away and never returned.

Stephen lived in North Adams, Mass.

Jerusha M. John Kyle, lives in the West.

Goodell Walker first built on the place where Charles Russell lives, but sold the place to Ira Russell, who came from Jamaica. He built the present house and most of the buildings, and greatly enlarged and improved the farm, living on it until he died in 1874, aged 76 years.

CHILDREN OF IRA RUSSELL.

Sally M. E. P. Luther of Dorset, both died in East Dorset.

Eunice M. Zeno Cone, lived in Winhall; died in 1885.

MRS. I. K. BATCHELDER.

Nahum M. Emma Benson of Dorset moved West; died there.

Samantha M. James Griffith of Mount Tabor, lives there.

Caroline M. Allen Benson, who died in Andersonville prison.

Charles M. Lucy Carter for his first wife, and Clarinda Lothrop for the second; lives in Peru.

George M. Laura Clayton for his first wife, and Widow Blakely for the second; lives in Peru.

Charles came into possession of the paternal farm, and now lives on it.

Edward Messenger came from Dedham, Mass., with Jesse Warren, and in 1829 bought of him half a lot of land west of the Russell farm, putting up all the buildings now on the farm. He was a carpenter and joiner by trade, and worked at the business the greater part of his time, working on the farm only in the busy season. He was an active, energetic man in business, a useful citizen, and genial in his family. In 1839 his parents came to live with him in their declining years, but his father lived only a short time, while his mother lived to the good old age of 96 years, always striving to make all around her happy, and happy with herself. Her son made her happy by giving her a good home and seeing that her wants were all supplied, and for no other remuneration than to do his filial duty and the rich reward he received for doing that. Edward Messenger died in 1876, aged 76 years; his wife died some time before.

CHILDREN OF EDWARD MESSENGER.

Mary M. Adam Corbet, lived in Peru; died in 1875.

Nancy M. James Pebbles, died young in Massachusetts.

Laura M. Riley Pebbles, died young in Massachusetts.

Sarah M. Henry Mellendy, died in Boston.

Ellen M. Henry Mellendy, lives in Chicago.

Lucius Messenger came from Wrentham, Mass., in 1829, and built a house on the lower side of the highway southwest of Edward Messenger's house. He soon sold out to Amherst Messenger and returned to Massachusetts. Amherst lived on the place, farming and shoemaking, until about 1850, when he returned to Massachusetts, the place going into Edward Messenger's hands. The house that stood on the place is gone.

CHILDREN OF AMHERST MESSENGER.

Emily M. Joseph Simonds, lived in Peru.

John B. M. Louisa Washburn, lives in Natick, Mass.

Horace Jackson came from Dedham, Mass., in 1830, and commenced new on a half lot west of E. Messenger's land, erecting the buildings and clearing the land. Mrs. Jackson was a valuable woman in society. They had two children, Edwin and Mary, who went with them to South Deerfield, Mass., in 1860, the farm being sold to P. H. Russell, who lived on it for some years and then sold it to Joshua Wilder. P. H. Russell moved to Arlington, where he buried his wife, and is now living in Michigan.

General Peter Dudley came into town in 1801, and settled on a lot south of Josiah Barnard's farm, building a log house near where the present buildings stand. It was not long before he had built the first two-story house in town, using split clapboards, shaved. He remained on the farm until his death, in 1847, when it went into the possession of his son, General Stephen Dudley, who remained on it some years, then selling out to Seth L. Walker, the present owner and resident.

CHILDREN OF GENERAL PETER DUDLEY.

Peter m. Delia Davis, lived in Manchester; died in 1882.

General Stephen m. Lydia Davis, lived in Peru and 'Derry; died in Andover.

Lucy married in western New York, died there.

Elvira married in western New York, died in Michigan.

Lydia m. David Arnold, lived in 'Derry; died in 1886.

James married in Johnstown, N. Y., lives there.

Samuel died young.

Sophia m. Nelson Curtis, lived in Hoosick, N. Y.

Caroline m. Charles Lee, died in Kentucky.

Damietta m. Mr. Bates, lived in Shaftsbury; died there.

Helen m. E. Holton, lives in Illinois.

CHILDREN OF GENERAL STEPHEN DUDLEY.

Myron married; is a clergyman, settled in Connecticut.

George went to Kentucky, died there.

Lucy m. P. J. Walker, died in Peru.

Elmer married, lives in Massachusetts.

Estelle m. Mr. Adams, lives in Chester.

Homer m. Miss Eames, lives in 'Derry.

Caroline married, lives in Andover.

Three of General Stephen Dudley's sons, Myron, Elmer and Homer, enlisted at the time of the rebellion. Elmer lost one of his limbs

MRS. DAVID SIMONDS

DEA. DAVID SIMONDS

Jesse Warren came into town in 1829 from Dedham, Mass., and purchased the Butterfield farm, containing four hundred acres of land. There was a large set of hotel buildings on the hill one-third of a mile north of the present buildings, on the old road. These buildings were located before the allotment of the town, being the first and only tavern from Utley's in Landgrove to Manchester. Mr. Warren moved the house down on to the turnpike, being the house he lived in. The basement he used for a shop. He and his son-in-law, Hiram Messenger, erected the large house and two large barns, and Mr. Messenger kept a hotel for fourteen years in the new house. Mr. Warren sold one hundred acres of his land to E. Messenger and H. Jackson, but carried on the farm and cleared some of the land, also manufacturing cast iron ploughs and castings for various purposes, as well as carrying on the blacksmith's business. He started this business on the top of the mountain, but the buildings are all taken down, there being no sign left of the first location. The hotel building still stands, but the rest of the buildings have been built since. Mr. Warren and his family coming to town at the time they did, their influence was good and elevating; he was a valuable citizen and always ready to lend a helping hand to every useful enterprise, besides doing much to build up and sustain society. He did much towards supporting the town schools, and it was here that his family of ten children received the rudiments of their education. Mr. Warren remained in town about eight or ten years and then went to Springfield, Vt., where he purchased a foundry and continued the business of making ploughs and castings.

CHILDREN OF JESSE WARREN.

Mary Ann M. Hiram Messenger, lived in Peru, but moved to Detroit, Mich.

Joseph M. Roxana Richardson, moved to Ohio; both dead.

Betsey M. B. S. Ballard, died on Long Island.

Elvira M. Mr. Bisbee, lives in Springfield, Vt.

Harriet took care of her mother in declining years at Fitchburg, Mass.

Joseph, the oldest son, worked at the same business as his father, settling down in Medina County, Ohio, where he has been successful and prosperous in his business. The other five brothers, whose names are John, Samuel M., Cyrus, Marshall and Burgess, have been in company, first in the cement roofing business in different cities in the North and Middle States, and have also been extensively engaged in refining petroleum at the Warren Chemical Works, Brooklyn, N. Y. It is said that the oil from these works is a superior article. Samuel entered the ministry, and lives in the vicinity of Boston; he married his wife in England. John withdrew from the company and settled near his brother Joseph in Ohio. Marshall was drowned by a collision on Long Island Sound. Cyrus is a chemist, and is settled down in Brookline, Mass., devoting his time to chemistry for the benefit of the company. He is connected with the Boston School of Technology. The Warren boys have been remarkably prosperous business men since they left Peru, and are in affluent circumstances, made so by their untiring energy and industry.

Dr. Silas Clark came into town from Winhall in 1809, and settled in a log house on the old road north of Charles Russell's house, being on the same lot, but did only a small amount of professional business. He was a useful member of society, and did much to build it up. Mrs. Clark died of typhoid fever about 1814, and Dr. Clark soon moved to Herkimer County, N. Y., selling the place to Goodell Walker in 1817.

The house west of Dr. Clark's on the old road, at the foot of the hill, was a log house, built by Mr. Butler, of whom nothing is known. This lot of land belongs to the Russell farm at this time.

Jonathan Butterfield came to Peru about 1795, and previous to the allotment of the town. He made a pitch on the height of land in the south part of the town, about one hundred rods from Winhall line, building a large house, barn, and sheds, convenient for a hotel. Mr. Lovel was associated with him in erecting these buildings. Mr. Butterfield kept a public-house for some years, it being known as the Butterfield tavern far and near. In 1810 Mr. Cooper was landlord for some years, then Mendal Fosgot run it for a time, after which Jeduthan Bruce had it, he being the last landlord of the house. The turnpike was completed in 1816, and travelers left the old road for the new one. Hiram Messenger opened a public-house in a new building on the turnpike road in 1831 or '32, and kept it ten or twelve years, when the place, with the Warren farm, went into the hands of Mr. Briggs. Alexander Leland leased the tavern for a short time and run it as a hotel. J. G. Mellendy came to town with a large family, and bought the property of Mr. Briggs, but took the hotel sign down after being there a year. It was next sold to Seth H. Dickinson, whose family own the property at the present time.

Mr. Mellendy had a large family of children, and took great pride in educating them and helping to sustain the school, and his three eldest daughters were excellent school teachers. He moved to Deerfield, Mass., in 1858, and died there in 1883.

CHILDREN OF J. G. MELLENDY.

Emily M. Mr. Putnam, lived in Cleveland until her husband's death, now living in South Deerfield.

Orrilla M. Stephen Grout, lived in East Dorset; died there.

Ella M., lived in Boston; died there.

Henry M. Sarah Messenger for his first wife, who died in Boston, and Ellen Messenger for his second.

The younger members of the family are some east and some west.

Jesse Brown married Sally Brooks and came from Princeton to Peru in 1803, beginning on the farm where his son Jesse now resides, and built a log house and barn. He and his son Jesse built the buildings now on the farm, the latter keeping the paternal acres. Asa, Jesse's son, takes care of his father and mother and inherits the estate, so keeping the place in the name of the Browns for three generations. Jesse Brown died in 1860, aged 92 years, and his wife in 1854, aged 81 years.

CHILDREN OF JESSE BROWN, SEN.

Sally M. Hinckley Cook, who died in Peru in 1865. At the time of Mrs. Cook's death in 1889 she was the oldest person in town, being 96 years old.

John M Bathsheba Trash, died in Peru.

Jesse M. Elizabeth Hapgood for his first wife, she died in Peru in 1834; his second wife was Mary Ann Everett, died in Peru in 1853; his third wife was Hannah Whitney, lives in Peru. Jesse died in 1889, aged about 90 years.

Dr. Asa B. M. in Ohio; died in 1844, aged 37 years.

John Brown built the buildings where his son Justus lives, and who owns the farm, he being the only child. Justus married Irene Walker, the widow of Duane Walker.

Deacon David Simonds, son of Elijah Simonds, was born in Gardner, Mass., in 1786, and moved to Peru in 1802. He married Anna Byam of Jaffrey, N. H., in 1810, and died at New Ipswich, July 12, 1869, aged 83 years. Mrs. Simonds died in Peru in 1885, aged 94 years.

CHILDREN OF DAVID SIMONDS.

Sarah Ann died young, October 11, 1835.

David K. died young, June 24, 1835.

Oliver P. M. Mary A. Cone, lives in Peru.

Joseph H. M. Emily Messenger, died at Peru in 1876.

Amanda M. Deacon Frost, lives in New Ipswich, N. H.

Stephen D. M. Emeline Carter for his first wife, and Ellen Stiles for the second, lives in Granville, Ill.

Elmina M. Milo Simpson, lives in Hoosick, N. Y.

Elijah M. Angeline Eddy, died at Peru in 1866.

Edwin B. M. Marian Farnum, lives in Virginia.

Affa A. M. James Pebbles, lives in New Ipswich, N. H.

David K. M. Ellen Clark, lives in Manchester, Vt.

O. P. Simonds, of the above family, has lived in Peru all his life excepting two years, when he worked on a farm in Wallingford. He has worked at shoemaking for fifty years, been town clerk and postmaster for forty-three years, member of the legislature two terms, and succeeded his father as deacon of the church, which office he has held about thirty-eight years. Joseph Simonds was a farmer, and a useful man in town and society. Stephen is also a prosperous farmer in Granville, Ill. David is a lawyer by profession, but is now editor of the Manchester Journal, is town clerk, and has been a member of the upper and lower houses in the legislature.

Sylvanius Densmore began on a lot east of the David Simonds place, and put up some buildings. He stayed on this place some years and moved away. Scammel Burt then occupied the premises until 1823, when the house was burnt. Mr. Burt built a house at the foot of the hill near Stowell Barnard's.

Zimri Whitney began on the Nourse farm, building a shanty and barn, but sold out to Mr. Thompson of 'Derry, who was killed on the place by a falling tree. Benjamin Barnard then bought the place, but keeping it only two years, when he sold it to Joel Nourse, who greatly improved the buildings and farm, living on it until he moved to Grafton, where he died. The farm is still owned by the Nourse family.

CHILDREN OF JOEL NOURSE.

Adaline M. A. Davenport, lived in Chester.

A. C. M. Sarah Stiles, lives in Grafton.

Nathaniel Gates began new on the Cook place, but sold out to Mr. Adams, he selling the place to Hinckley Cook, who died on the place in 1865. Mrs. Cook continued to live on the place. She died in 1889, aged 90 years.

Sally M. Isaac Cochran, lived in Winhall; died in Kansas.

Amanda lives at home, unmarried.

Lydia M. Mr. Hamilton, lived in Winhall, moved to Michigan.

Martin lives on the paternal farm, unmarried.

Daniel Wood commenced on the place where his son John lives. They built the house and barn and cleared the land. Daniel and his wife died on the farm at a good old age. John is still living on the farm.

Thomas Wyman bought the land where Royal Bryant's house stands, with all the land in M. B. Lyon's pasture, in 1832, and built the house on it. In 1839 he sold the place to Francis Bennett, and about that time O. P. Simonds bought the house with four acres of land from him. Mr. Simonds occupied the place for some time, then sold it again to Francis Bennett in 1842, who kept a small store in the west end of the house for two years and built a small barn. In 1845 Thomas French bought the premises, rented them a year, and then moved on to the place himself, remaining some years. Dr. D. H. Marden bought the premises in 1850, built an addition to the barn and improved the place in every respect. He sold the place to Royal Bryant, who built the blacksmith shop, repaired and painted the house. J. G. Walker bought the place from him. Royal Bryant was a strong, muscular man, he lived in many different places in town, and worked out a good deal in order to support his family. He would sometimes imbibe a little too much, but was a good hunter and fisher, and never forgot his gun when he started for a tramp on Sunday morning. Later in life he changed his course, and instead of taking his gun and fish pole on Sunday morning, he carried his Bible and went with his wife to church, where he could unite in spirit with those who were singing the songs of Zion. He had a family of ten children, six boys and four girls. Four of his stalwart sons volunteered for service in the Union army, two serving three years in the Army of the Potomac, one was killed, and the other one served until he was mustered out at the close of the war. Mr. Bryant furnished more soldiers than any other family in town. He died in Massachusetts in 1889, and his wife died in 1881.

George M., lives in Texas.

Clark M., lives in Massachusetts.

Cynthia M. Asa Philips, who died in the army.

Angeline M. Mr. Brown, lives in Massachusetts.

Warren lives in Texas.

Leroy enlisted and was killed in battle.

Calvin M. Nancy Simonds, daughter of Oscar Simonds, lived in Peru, now in Pennsylvania.

George was in Texas when the war commenced, and was compelled to join the Confederate army.

Thomas Wyman, jr., bought the place near the school house, on which he lived about forty years, from his brother Parker, who built the house. Thomas made additions to the house, built the barn, and cultivated more land. This piece of land was part of Deacon Wyman's farm. Person T. Wyman now owns and occupies this place, and it is hoped he will improve it as much as his father did, and that four stocks will grow where two did under his father's cultivation.

Mark Batchelder built the house in which A. T. Byard lives in 1841, and lived in it until he died, in 1863. He built the barn and shop, where he worked at blacksmithing. In 1872 his widow, Rooxby Batchelder, sold the place to A. T. Byard.

CHILDREN OF MARK BATCHELDER.

Jane M. Royal Manley of Dorset, died some years ago.

Martha M. C. F. Long, lived in Manchester, Dorset, and Detroit, Mich.; died in 1889.

John L. M. Rachel Slocum of Factory Point, lives in Detroit, Mich.

Mahala M. Baker Wilson of Dorset, lives at Factory Point.

O. P. Simonds erected his house in 1841, where, with the exception of a year or two that he lived in Wallingford, he has lived since.

CHILDREN OF O. P. SIMONDS.

Francis M. Martha George, lives in Natick, Mass., now in Chicago.

Sarah Ann M Platt Quackenboss for her first husband. He died in the war. She then married O. N. Russell. He died in Arlington.

Mary M. Lysander Russell, lived in Natick, Mass.

Jane M. Charles H. Bean, died in Lawrence, Mass.

Urial M. Emma Simmonds, lives in Natick, Mass.

J. B. Simonds is a musician, unmarried, lives in Brattleboro.

The house where W. Whitney lives was built by J. J. Hapgood in 1843, Ruel Gibson being the first one to live in it. George Batchelder bought it of Mr. Hapgood, and lived in it a few years, then selling it to W. Whitney, who built the out-buildings.

CHILDREN OF W. WHITNEY.

Louise, unmarried, lives with her father.

Charles M. Matilda Baker of Danby, lived in Peru.

Josiah H. M. Mary Jane Walker, lived in Peru.

J. J. Hapgood bought his land of Joseph Barnard in 1827, and built all the buildings on the place. The Tuthill hotel was the only building near the place at the time. Mr. Hapgood was a builder, trader and farmer up to the time of his death in 1877.

CHILDREN OF J. J. HAPGOOD.

Charlotte, unmarried, a music teacher in Cambridge, Mass.

Luke B. M. Ellen Davis of Peru. He was one of the firm of L. B. & J. J. Hapgood, doing mercantile business in Peru until 1870, when he went into the shoe business in Boston, residing in North Cambridge, but is now in the shoe business in Easton, Mass.

Charles M., lives in Easton, Penn.

Marshall J. M. Flora Higgins of Dorset; he owns the old homestead in Peru, and does a large mercantile and lumbering business.

Wm. E. Polly built a store east of the parsonage house about 1854, and traded in it three or four years, when he closed up the business and left the place. John Q. Adams bought the building and made it into a dwelling house about 1876, C. W. Whitney living in it for a time. John Q. Adams owned and occupied it at the time it was burnt.

The brick tavern was built in 1822 by Daniel and Russell Tuthill of Landgrove. This is the only brick house in town, and is thoroughly built for a public house of bricks made in Deacon Wyman's brickyard. Esquire Tuthill opened the house to the public in the autumn of 1822, and it has been used as a hotel for more than sixty years. It had a large run of custom until 1850, when the railroads began to divert the travel and freight in other directions. Esquire Tuthill and his son Russell knew how to keep a good public house, and they did it, which secured for them a large patronage until they sold out to Lawrence McMullen in 1836. The family moved to Southern Illinois, and consisted of Esquire Daniel Tuthill and wife, Russell and wife and three children, Sally, who married Thomas Ross, Betsey Purdy, old lady Tuthill's daughter, and Silas, the youngest in the family. Silas is manufacturing chairs on the banks of the Mississippi river. They had to endure all the hardships incident to settling a new country, being so far south that they did not have any market for their produce, and were completely isolated from the outside world. On the opening of the Illinois Central railroad they had the means to be connected with all the world, and a great blessing it was to them. Russell moved to Duquoin, where he and his family had all needful advantages. Esquire Tuthill and his wife died soon after settling in Illinois, and · Thomas Ross and his wife lived but a few years. Russell and Miss Purdy are both dead. It was a great loss to Peru to lose this family, and no one has come to fill the vacant place.

Lawrence McMullen bought the hotel of Esquire Tuthill in 1836, and carried it on some years, building the east addition. He rented it to Mr. Smalley, who run it two or three years. Freeman Lyon rented the place several years at different times, and Hiram Messenger a year or two. Mr. McMullen sold the place to Charles Lyon, who kept it a short time, selling out to Ruel Gibson, who run it two years. He sold the place to Leonard Howard, who kept it several years, when Edward Batchelder bought and run it for a time, selling it to G. K. Davis, who now owns and occupies it, going by the name of the Bromley House. If you want a good dinner this is the place to get it.

John Chandler, whose wife was a half sister to Deacon Wyman, came into town from Princeton in 1801, and commenced new on the farm now owned by Wallace West. He cleared it of the forest and built the first house and barn. Mr. Chandler was a farmer and a mechanic, making the best of hand rakes, and turned the bows and teeth with a foot lathe. He sold the place to Jonathan Walker, who occupied it for a time, but sold out to Freeman Lyon, who lived on the place a few years. Simeon Lyon owned it and lived there about four years, then selling to Charles Lyon, who sold out to Lawrence McMullen, who died on the farm in 1850. Charles Batchelder owned and lived on this place some years, but sold out to S. B. Russell, who rented it to Rev. A. G. Bowker. Mr. Russell sold the place to Nathan Lillie, who improved the buildings and sold out to Wallace West, the present occupant.

CHILDREN OF JOHN CHANDLER.

Mary m. James Lincoln, died in 1843 at Peru.

Dorcas m. Lawrence McMullen for her first husband, and David Garfield for her second; died in Landgrove in 1889.

Mabel m. Simeon Lyon, lives in New York State.

Eunice m. Barney Richardson, lives in Manchester.

Mrs. J. J. Hapgood

J. J. HAPGOOD

Sally died young in Peru.

Harriet M. Amos Lawrence, lived in Manchester; died in February, 1885.

Ezra M. Elizabeth English of Hartland, lived in Peru; died in November, 1885.

CHILDREN OF E. P. CHANDLER.

Clarence M. Mary Lombra of Connecticut. He was a chip of the old block in mechanical ingenuity, having been employed as a scientific mechanic in Providence, R. I. He died in 1889.

Aden M. Isa Ackley of Bennington, Vt.; he is foreman in a newspaper office in Meriden, Conn.

Mary M. Henry C. Lombra, lives in Springfield, Mass.

William Green, Sen., came from Princeton, Mass., and began new where the James Lincoln house stands, and built a log house. He was one of the early settlers. Mrs. Green died about 1814, and he returned from whence he came, taking his youngest son with him. William, an older son, married Dorcas Lyon, and remained on the farm until 1830, when he sold out to James Lincoln. Mr. Green and his family, which was quite large, left town and went to Ohio, but returned two different times. He lived for a while in the old house on the parsonage lot, near M. B. Lyon's place, and afterwards began on a wild lot west of B. Barnard's place, where he built a log house. He went west again and settled down. James Lincoln lived on this place until he died in 1882, aged 74 years. He was a hard working, industrious, useful man, and did more work for other people than any other man in town. He stuck the corner of an adze into his knee, which caused him to have a stiff knee and almost cost him his life. His first wife was Mary Chandler, who died in 1844, leaving seven children; his second wife was Syble Hale, who died in 1866, leaving three children; he married the third wife, who died before he did.

Elisha Whitney was one of the first settlers, and came from Westminster. He began on the Gould farm, building his log house in the pasture north from the present buildings. He was a good citizen and a member of the church. Both he and his wife died about 1816. Four children came to Peru with them.

CHILDREN OF ELISHA WHITNEY.

Joseph M. Hannah Towns of Andover.

Sally M. Cyrus Staples, lived in Peru; died there.

Tryphosa, unmarried, died in Putney at her brother Norman's.

Norman M. Belinda Batchelder of Landgrove, moved from Peru to Andover, then to Putney; died there.

Joseph inherited the homestead, and enlarged and improved the buildings. Living under the mountain he frequently had an opportunity to try his trusty rifle for the benefit of the bears, and those he could not shoot he caught in traps, being a terror to wild animals. He raised a large family, the oldest daughter marrying R. Stone in Peru. In 1835 Mr. Whitney emigrated to Ohio, settling near Oberlin with all his family, who have been remarkably prosperous. Joseph Howard bought the place and lived on it until he died in 1843, when his son Leonard lived on the farm several years, and then sold out to A. D. Lincoln, who kept it a year or two, Amos Batchelder then buying the place. James Farnum had what was south of the brook, but lived there only a few years, selling out to Horace Gould, who occupied it until he died in 1878. Ira Wait next bought the place, and resides on it at the present time.

CHILDREN OF H. GOULD.

Horace, unmarried, died in 1837.

Lucia, unmarried, lives in Peru.

Emily M. Shepherd Aldrich, lives in Peru.

Sullivan, unmarried, lived in Peru; died in 1887.

The farm on which M. B. Lyon resides was first begun by Wm. Barlow in 1773, but very little is known of him. It is supposed that he died in town and was buried in the corner of the Holton lot. The first house known on the place stood below the road north of the gate, the foundations still remaining. It was a house of some dimensions, and evidently put up at different times. More families have lived in this house than in any other in town. The first that we know of was Joseph Fairbanks, who lived on the place from 1805 until 1812; Isaac Hill occupied it a short time; Deacon Benjamin Ballard lived there a short time; Warren Wyman occupied it for the first store in town; Mr Bryant, a blacksmith, lived in it about 1822. These occupied the place as tenants, David Brooks being the owner. He sold out to Peter Allen, who carried on the farm a few years. Freeman Lyon lived on this place in our time. Joseph Howard came from Athol, Mass., about 1825, and bought the farm from Peter Allen. He and his family lived in the old house until 1833, when he built a new one. In 1838 he sold the place to Francis Bennett, who built an L. to the house and moved the middle barn from L. Wyman's farm to its present location. I. K. Batchelder then bought the place and moved on to it in the spring of 1840. He moved the L. for a shed and shop, put up a new L., and finished the house as it is at the present time, painting it white; he also built the sheds to the barns and moved the south barn to its present location. In 1869 he sold the place to M. B. Lyon, who now occupies it.

CHILDREN OF JOSEPH HOWARD.

Louisa, went to Ohio, died there.

Harriet M., went to Illinois, died there.

Hiram studied medicine and settled in Ohio; died in 1880.

Leonard M. Betsey Gibson, died at Derry in 1881.

Olivet settled in Pittsburg, Penn. Married there.

Joseph died in New York State.

Jonathan lives in East Dorset. Married there.

Sylphronia and Silas went to Illinois when young.

The house near M. B. Lyon's was built for a parsonage about 1837. William Green owned the place and lived in the old house. The Congregational society bought it about 1833, and Rev. Mr. Parsons assisted in paying for it. Rev. Mr. Baldwin was minister at the time, and did much of the work on the house, living in it until 1846. His successor, Rev. A. S. Swift, lived there about three years, and Rev. A. F. Clark two years. J. J. Hapgood had the house in part payment for building the new parsonage, and several families lived in it as his tenants. He sold the place to Widow Roxana Dale, who occupied it a few years and then sold out to Widow Nancy Banks, she living in it until 1867, when she sold the place to Widow Mary Barnard, who afterwards married Edward Messenger, both dying there. A large number of families have lived in this house since Mrs. Dale bought it of Mr. Hapgood. Old Mr. Fisher died here about 1850. The present owner and occupant is John Q. Adams.

The farm on which Dexter and Robert Batchelder live was begun in 1795 by the Stratton family, of whom very little is known. Lady Stratton died at the house of Jonathan Walker, who was one of the family, about 1825. The Strattons deeded the north cemetery to the town in 1803. Jacob Odell of Mount Vernon, N. H., bought the farm of Richard and David Stratton, and erected a frame house. He deeded the common to the town, on which the first church was built. Mr. Odell did not live on this place, but sold it to Nathan Whitney, who came from Athol, Mass., in 1819, with a large family. Mr. Whitney was a man of great energy and push, and would make things boom. He finished the house and made great improvements on the farm. Being a carpenter by trade, he framed and finished many buildings in the town. He was constable for many years In 1836 he sold out to Peter Dudley, Jr., and emigrated to Pittsfield, Ohio. Mr. Dudley lived on the place three years, then sold out to Jonas Bennett, who came from Boston in 1839, he living on it until 1842. Jonas Bennett sold the farm to Aaron Burton, who occupied it several years, improving the farm. Jesse Rider then bought and occupied it until after the war, when he sold out to Wesley Woodward, who lived on the place until 1871, and then sold it to Dexter Batchelder, the present occupant. He has made great improvements in the buildings and farm.

CHILDREN OF NATHAN WHITNEY.

Alvah M. Lydia Heald of Chester, moved to Ohio; died in 1888.

Ira M. Susan Thurston, moved to Pittsfield, Ohio; died there.

Ann M. S. W. Lincoln of Peru, moved to Oberlin, Ohio.

William M. Persis Hapgood, lived in Peru; died in 1888.

Louisa M., lived in Ohio; died there.

Lucina M., lives in Ohio.

Elmira M., lives in Ohio.

Lucinda M., lives in Ohio.

Nathan and George moved to Ohio.

Isaac Bigelow commenced new on the farm now owned by J. P. Long, building a log house and barn on the spot where the new house is built at the forks of the road. He came from Westminster, Mass., and was a man of good ability intellectually. It is said that he was not very fond of work, and of course if the soil was not cultivated and sown, it did not produce very abundantly. He sold the place to Joseph Stone in 1819, and moved to Pawlet with a large family.

The old farm of Dexter Batchelder was begun new by Marshall Bigelow, who came from Westminster, Mass., and was one of the early settlers. He was a very superior singer. Mr. Bigelow built a small house south-west from the Chase factory, and then sold out to Israel Batchelder, emigrating to Granville, Ohio. Israel Batchelder came to town in 1809, and lived on his farm until he died in 1858, aged 77 years. This farm was mostly covered with hard wood timber, the soil was strong and very productive when first cleared. He built the large two-story house in 1816. Dexter and Robert Batchelder are the present owners.

CHILDREN OF ISRAEL BATCHELDER.

Mary Jane M. Joel Lyon, lived in Peru; died in 1889.

Abigail M. Joel Adams, lived in Peru; died in 1880.

Nancy M. James Curtis, lived in East Dorset; died in 1886.

George M. Elvira Peck of Royalston, Mass.; died in East Dorset.

Edward M. Harriet Wyman, lives in East Dorset; his wife died there.

Susan M. Ira Cochran, died in East Dorset in 1883.

Dexter M. Susan Bloomer of Dorset, lived in Peru; died in March, 1888.

Margarette M. Joseph Griswold, lives in Bellows Falls.

John M. Frances Sayles, lived in Detroit, Mich. Died in 1890.

The place on which Amos Batchelder lives was begun by Capt. James Lincoln in 1818, who came from Keene, N. H. He built some of the buildings and lived on the place until 1844, when he sold it to his son Amos and moved to Michigan. Amos Lincoln built the large barn and shed. In 1850 he sold the place to Amos Batchelder, the present occupant, and moved on to the Smith farm, where he died of consumption.

CHILDREN OF CAPT. JAMES LINCOLN.

James M. Mary Chandler, lived in Peru; died in 1882, aged 74 years.

Stillman W. M. Ann Whitney, moved to Oberlin, Ohio; died in 1882, aged 72 years.

William B. studied medicine, moved to Ionia, Mich., in 1834; died in 1882, aged 70 years.

Prentice M., settled in the west.

Amos D. M. Olive Mann of Dover; he died in Peru in 1854, aged 41 years.

Lucy married in Michigan, died there.

Henry M. in Pittsfield, Ohio. He enlisted in the army and went to the war; died there.

Chauncey M., lived in Michigan.

Dexter M. in Michigan, lives there.

The farm Edgar Batchelder lives on was begun early by Philemon Parker, who came from Westmoreland, N. H. He built a log house on the corner of the lot north of the road that leads to Mr. Bell's place. In 1812 his family were all sick with what was called the spotted fever. Mrs. Dr. Whiting, who at that time was only fifteen years of age, and two or three other persons, watched over the sick ones. The children all died in the order they were born: Jonas, aged 24 years; Nathan, aged 22 years; Susan, aged 20 years; Anna, aged 18 years. Mrs. Parker had the fever and died soon after. Philemon Parker sold the place to Joseph Barnard and went to Westmoreland. Henry Whitney came from Athol, Mass., bought the place from Joseph Barnard, and built the house and barn now on the place. In 1830 he sold it to Alvah Whitney and moved to Walpole, N. H. Alvah sold it to his brother, Ira Whitney, who sold it to W. W. Whitney. The Farnums bought it from him in 1840, and lived on the farm until 1881, when it was sold to Edgar Batchelder, the present owner and occupant.

David Smith came from Marlboro, Mass., in 1804, and began on the farm where Mr. Bell now lives, clearing the land and erecting the buildings. He was a strong, athletic man, and could tell the biggest story of any man in the crowd. He lived on the farm until 1828, when he sold it to Jonathan Walker, who kept it a few years and then sold it to Capt. James Lincoln. He sold part of the land and buildings to Mr. Follansbee, who improved the buildings and sold the place to A. D. Lincoln. He died on the farm and his widow sold out to C. F. Morrill, who lived on it a few years and then sold to Mr. Hazzeton, he selling it to Joel Bell, who occupies it at this time.

CHILDREN OF DAVID SMITH.

Martin was a tanner and went to Pawlet to live.

David was educated for a teacher; his whereabouts are not known.

Oliver is a shoemaker; he is married and lives in Massachusetts.

Abigail and Nathaniel went to Marlborough, Mass., with their parents in 1828.

Jonas Stone commenced on the Rollins farm about 1827, built a log house, but did not clear much of the land. In 1830 he sold the place to Joseph Rollins, who came from Swanzey, N. H. He erected the buildings and cleared the land, having a good grass farm. Augustus Albee, from Rockingham, next bought the place, and lived on it until he sold it to Barnard & Gibson, who sold it to Elder Stevens. Rev. Amos Bowker carried on the farm several years for Mr. Stevens, who sold it to the present owner, Samuel Stiles.

Elijah Carlton and his brother began on the lot west of the

Rollins farm, where they built a log house and barn, but only lived on it a year or two. They sold the place to J. J. Hapgood and left town. No one has lived on the place since.

In 1819 Mr. Harris, who came from Springfield, cleared about 20 acres on the lot north of the Rollins farm, but did not move on to it. Willis Aldrich, from 'Derry, built a house and barn on this lot in 1835. He sold the place to Charles Barnard and Mr. Gibson, who sold it to T. J. Lakin in 1850. After he had built a new barn he sold out to Sarel Sawyer, who occupied it for a long time. It is now in the hands of J. P. Long. Elijah Carlton came from New Hampshire and married Maria, daughter of Jonas Bennett, who died, leaving two daughters. He then married Mary Long, and is now living in 'Derry.

CHILDREN OF WILLIS ALDRICH.

Shepherd M. Emily Gould, lives in Peru.

Hiram M. Miss S. Bennett, moved away.

There was another daughter who went west.

Jacob Bennett built a log house on the lot west of the Sawyer place in the woods, but did not clear the land. He lived in the house a few years and then left, no one living in the house since. Mr. Bennett was a mason by trade, and several of his sons have excelled in that business.

Horace Gould commenced on the Sawyer place about 1837, and built a log house and barn. In 1840 he built a saw mill, placing it where the present one stands. He sold the place to John Sawyer in 1846, who built the present house in 1848. In 1850 all the family had the typhus fever, Harvey, the oldest, being the first one down, but they all took it one after another. Mr. Sawyer was taken sick and died in October. They had been a strong, healthy family previous to this, but it left them consumptive. After his death Mrs. Sawyer, with the help of the boys, carried on the farm and built the present barn. A few years later Mrs. Sawyer deeded her right in the farm to her son John, he agreeing to pay the debts and maintain his mother. John soon sold his share to his brother Sarel, with the encumbrances on the farm, Sarel agreeing to fulfill all John's obligations. Mrs. Sawyer died in 1871, aged 76 years.

CHILDREN OF JOHN SAWYER.

Harvey died of typhus fever, aged 21 years.

John M. Sarah McClennan, lives in California.

Sarel m. Jane Conable, lives in Peru.

Ambrose m. Ellen Hill, died in Chittenden, buried at Peru.

Hannah m. Thomas Cross of California, died in Peru on July 13th, 1871, aged 35 years.

Ann m. Charles Morrill, died in Peru in 1875, aged 35 years.

Harlan died of typhus fever in 1850, aged 11 years.

Seth died in Peru of consumption in 1871, aged 24 years.

Edward married in New Hampshire, died there of consumption.

The farm on which Samuel Stiles lives is a lease lot, first division drawn to the school right. Samuel Bruce, who came from Westminster, took a lease of this lot from the town, agreeing to pay a stipulated rent every year to support the schools. He was an early settler, and built a log house and barn. In 1817 he sold the betterments to Peter A. Gould, who came from Wrentham, Mass., and returned to Westminster. Mr. Gould was a revolutionary pensioner. He and his son Horace lived on the place until 1822, when they sold the betterments to Jonas Bennett, who came from Groton, Mass., with his family. He built a frame house and barn, and lived on the place until his wife died, when he sold out to the Long brothers and moved over the mountain. Francis K. Stiles bought the place of the Longs, taking possession in 1850. He improved the farm and the buildings very much, and deeded the place to his son Samuel, who built the fine house now standing there.

CHILDREN OF JONAS BENNETT.

Jonas m. Ann Byard, lived in Manchester; died in 1863.

Albert m. Hepsibah Lyon, moved out west; died there.

Ann Maria m. Elijah Carlton, died in Peru.

Jane m. William Wiley of Landgrove, died there.

Samuel m. Miss Tryon, lives in Manchester.

Gilbert m., moved north.

Saviah m. Hiram Aldrich, moved away.

Loten m., lives in Goshen.

Daniel m. Sarah Fitch, lives in Winchenden.

Peter A. Gould moved on to the south half of the lease lot, west of the Smith lot, put up some buildings, and lived there until he died. His pension supported him in his last days. Both he and his wife lived to be very old.

The lot north of the Stiles farm is a lease lot, and was taken by Jeduthan Bruce, one of the early settlers, who built a log house and

MRS. ASA SIMONDS

ASA SIMONDS

barn on the place. He had a large family of children, whose names were Susannah, Polly, Mark, Jeduthan, and Betsey. In 1815 he sold the place to Ebenezer Stiles and moved into the Moses Killam house, where he died of a cancer in the face in 1816. The family moved to Lunenburg, Mass. After a lapse of more than fifty years his daughter, Polly Houghton, came back to Peru and had a suitable monument erected over her father's grave. Ebenezer Stiles built a new house and barn, improved the farm in every way, and sold out to Rev. Nathaniel Rawson in 1826, who lived on the place several years. He sold the place to Abel Larkin, who died there, Susan Larkin renting the farm to Gilman Temple. J. P. Long next owned the farm, but sold it to P. H. Russell. Nathan Brown bought it from Mr. Russell and lived there several years, when he sold out to Ira Wait, the present owner.

Stephen Bennett and wife, parents of Francis and Jonas Bennett, came to Peru about 1823. He was a shoemaker by trade, but lived on a pension which he received for serving in the revolutionary war. The last part of his life he spent with his son Jonas, where he died.

Moses Bruce was an early settler, and took a lease of the lot north of Ira Wait's farm, where he built a log house and barn, cleared the land and planted an orchard. In 1817 he sold the place to David Sawyer and went to Westminster, Mass. David Sawyer was a shoemaker by trade; he had been a soldier in the revolutionary war, for which he drew a pension. He sold out to his son John in 1828 and moved to Westford, Vt. John Sawyer lived on the farm until 1847, when he sold it to Horace Gould, who lived on it several years, and took care of his mother in her last days. Mrs. Gould lived to be very old. Horace Gould sold the place to Nathan Lillie and moved to the J. Whitney farm. George Reed next bought the farm, and is the present occupant. The rent of this land is paid to the Episcopal church.

CHILDREN OF DAVID SAWYER.

David M., lived in Mount Tabor, a mile from any neighbor.

Hannah M. Joseph Farnum, moved to Wells, N. Y.

Judith M. Moody Roby, lived in Peru; died about 1830.

Eliza, unmarried, died in Weston.

John M. Hannah Roby of Wilton, N. H.; she died in 1871, aged 72 years.

Alfred and Mary went to Westford with their parents.

Thomas French began new on the lot west of the Sawyer farm, cleared it and built good buildings. He sold the farm to his son Alonzo, who sold it to J. P. and C. F. Long. They sold the place to Nathan Lillie, who came from Dorset with his family. He sold out to Daniel Roby, who carried on the farm a short time and then sold it to Rufus Lake. About this time the buildings were burnt down, and have never been replaced.

Ebenezer Stiles was born in Wilton, N. H., in 1765, and his wife was born in Temple, N. H., in 1766. They were married at Temple in 1793, living in Wilton until 1800, when they moved to Landgrove, Vt. He enlisted in the army at the time of the war in 1812. They moved to Peru in 1813 and bought the lease lot from Jeduthan Bruce. Mr. and Mrs. Stiles were members of the Congregational church, and frequently had religious meetings at their house. At the anniversary of Mrs. Stiles's one hundreth birthday a large number of relatives and townspeople assembled at the house, where Rev. M. A. Gates administered the Lord's supper, which pleased the old lady very much. There were four generations living in the house at one time. Mr. Stiles died on September 24th, 1857, aged 92 years, and his wife on September 30th, 1868, aged 102 years and 6 months.

CHILDREN OF EBENEZER STILES.

Sarah M. Samuel Parker in 1820, died in New York State in 1867.

Polly M. Joseph Stone of Peru in 1828, died at Peru in 1879.

Ebenezer M. Clarissa Edson in 1826, died in New York State in 1865.

Alice, unmarried, died in 1876.

Francis K. M. Martha Stone of Peru in 1829, died in 1881.

Aaron M. Laura Irish of New York State, lives there.

Benjamin M. Lydia Cotten, died in New York State in 1868.

The lot west of the Ira Wait farm was commenced in 1820 by Ebenezer Stiles, Jun., who erected a house and a log barn. He sold the place to his father in 1826, who sold it to his son Francis. He improved the farm and buildings very much, doing more hard work on the side of the mountain than any man ought to do anywhere. Francis Stiles kept a large stock of cattle, and made large quantities of butter, hiring a great deal of help. In 1850 he bought the Bennett farm at the foot of the hill and moved on to it, leaving the old place, which no one has since lived on, to grow wild. In 1877.

he and his son Samuel, who now owns the paternal pastures, built a large two-story house, where Mr. and Mrs. Stiles spent their declining years. Their golden wedding was celebrated by their relatives and friends in 1879, when Rev. M. Scott read a poem, Rev. Wm. F. Gillis made a short speech, and Mary Chandler read a selection. Francis K. Stiles died in 1881, aged 78 years. Mrs. Francis Stiles, whose maiden name was Martha Stone, still lives; has always been a leader in society, living a life of active industry and toil. She has long been an active Christian in the church of the living God.

CHILDREN OF FRANCIS K. STILES.

Ellen M. S. D. Simonds, lived in Granville, Ill.; died in 1890.

Rosette M. M. G. Walker, lives in Manchester.

Henry M. Helen Rider, lives in Masonville, Iowa.

Sarah M. A. C. Nourse, lives in Grafton.

Samuel M. Sarah D. Conable of Bernardston, Mass.; she died in 1878, aged 32 years. Samuel M. Hattie A. Conable of Bernardston, Mass., for his second wife, lives in Peru.

Previous to 1820 Capt. James Lincoln built a log house on the lot north of Moody Roby's place, where he lived a year or two. In 1848 his son Prentice built a new house and lived there a short time.

John W. Farnum and Jonas Bennett began on a lot south of Moody Roby's farm about 1837, built a log house and barn and cleared some of the land. They sold the place in 1840 to Thomas French, who sold it to his son Joseph. Daniel Simpson next bought the place and built a frame house, carrying on the farm several years, when he sold out to Zimri Lathrop. Isaac Rush now owns the place.

The lot of land east of Moody Roby's farm was commenced by Mr. Blodgett, who was one of the early settlers. He sold the place to C. and E. Guillo, who built a log house and lived in it several years, when Isaac Rush took possession and erected good buildings, making it a good farm.

Stuart Lillie built a house north of George Reed's, in which he lived several years, when he left town.

A house was erected north of the Stuart Lillie house, and has been occupied by Frank Jones and several other families.

Henry Tifft came to town about 1860, bought a piece of land north of Frank Jones's place and built a small house. He was a shingle maker by trade, and a hard working, industrious man. He still lives on the place.

Moody Roby came from Nashua, N. H., in 1818, and settled on his farm in the woods. He had no neighbor north or west of him, was three miles to the nearest house on the east, and one mile to David Sawyer's on the south. He enlisted in the army at the time of the war in 1812, being only 16 years old at the time, and served six months. Mr. Roby married Judith Sawyer for his first wife, who died in 1831, when he married Dolly Richardson, who died in 1872. He died at the residence of his daughter in Manchester in 1883, aged 88 years.

CHILDREN OF MOODY ROBY.

David S. M. Phebe Grant of Massachusetts, died there.

Louisa A. M. George Q. A. Bryant, lives in Winchendon, Mass.

Mary B. M. William Emery, lives in New Hampshire.

Mahala M. Charles Morrell, died in New Hampshire.

David W. M. Jane Lampson, lives in Idaho.

Mariah S. M. Ralph Weston, lives in New Hampshire. ·

James Franklin, died.

An infant died.

Jane D. M. George Richardson, lives in Landgrove.

Hannah R. M. N. Fuller, lives in New York.

Betsey E. M. John Davis, lives in Manchester.

Allen S. M. Betsey Tuttle, lives in Springfield.

George, died young.

Amanda L. M. Richard Cook, lives in Manchester.

James F. M. Mary Lockwood, lives in Vermont.

Victoria H. M. Frank Jones, lives in Peru.

Shepherd Aldrich built all the buildings on his farm, being the first one that settled on the lot. He also built a mill in the north part of the town, which does some business. Mr. Aldrich married Emily Gould and has seven children. The farm is situated in one of the most sightly locations in town.

Samuel Stone came from Gardner, Mass., in 1802, and began on the farm where John Priest now lives. He was born in Gardner, Mass., in 1779, and was one of eleven children, all of whom grew up to marry and settle down in life. Samuel Stone married Susannah Haynes the same year that he came to Bromley. He commenced clearing the unbroken forest with strong hands and a determined will that overcame all obstacles, soon having a clearing large enough to build a log house. All the windows in the house were made of white paper, greased, and then pasted on to the sash. They lived in

H. O. DAVIS.

this house several years and then built the one now occupied by John Priest. Mr. Stone was a man who lent a willing hand in making improvements in a new country, such as making roads, building schoolhouses, and erecting churches. He was chosen to all the important offices of the town, was elected justice of the peace, sent as delegate to a constitutional convention, and was tythingman for a long time, which required him to see that the boys and girls who sat in the square boxes in the gallery sat up straight and gave reverent attention to the instructions proclaimed by the preacher in the high pulpit. The first time that Mr. and Mrs. Stone went to Gardner, Mrs. Stone rode horseback, while he accompanied her on foot. In the fall of 1825 the whole family, with the exception of Mrs. Stone, had the typhus fever, and one son died. In 1837 he sold the farm to James Bennett and went to Pittsfield, Ohio, where, with the help of one son, he cleared a farm and erected new buildings. It did not tend to lengthen his life by emigrating. He died in 1845, aged 66 years.

CHILDREN OF SAMUEL STONE.

Martha m. Francis K. Stiles, lives in Peru.

Samuel died in Peru of typhus fever in 1825.

Susan m. H. S. Farmer of Pittsfield, Ohio.

Reuben m. Hannah Whitney of Peru, moved to Pittsfield, Ohio, in 1835. He started for the west, with his young bride, in an emigrant wagon, carrying all he could, the most prominent being his axe and gun. He lived in Oberlin and died there in 1886.

Joseph m. in Ohio, died in 1854.

Willis m. Eliza Barnard, went to Ohio; died in 1848.

Betsey went to Ohio with her parents in 1842.

James Bennett lived on the Stone farm two years, then selling it to John Whitney, who came with his family from Rindge, N. H. He lived on the farm until Moses Priest bought it, when he moved back to Rindge. Mr. Priest died on this farm, and his son, John Priest, then took possession, occupying it at the present time.

CHILDREN OF MOSES PRIEST.

John D. m. Edith Scott of Mt. Tabor, lives in Peru.

Mahlon studied medicine, settled in New York as a physician and druggist.

Caroline lives in Plymouth.

Clarissa m. Amos Smith, settled in Weston.

Joseph Stone came from Gardner, Mass., in 1804, and lived with his brothers, Samuel and Josiah. He made cardboards, which were used for carding wool and tow in the domestic factories of the land, transporting his goods to Gardner by team. Uncle Joe would inspect the wilderness to find smooth beech, of which he made his cardboards, and no landmarks interfered with his right to do this. Mr. Stone married Polly Stiles in 1828, and moved on to the place which his children now occupy. He began new on this place, erected all the buildings and made the road. Mr. Stone died in 1856, aged 75 years, leaving three children, Harvey, Hezekiah and Lenora, who are all unmarried and living on the old homestead. Mrs. Stiles died in 1879.

Capt. Josiah Stone came from Gardner in 1808, and began on a new lot east of his brother Samuel's. He built the best log house in the town, it being made of peeled spruce, long and straight, nicely laid up, and all made square at the corners. The house had two large rooms, with a stone fireplace in the centre of each, and a comfortable chamber. The house was shingled, and the family occupied it about thirty years as it was first built. Capt. Stone soon had cultivated land in place of the forest, and planted an orchard, where he had a quantity of grafted fruit, which the boys would watch and sometimes take. It was not long before he commenced making sugar, at first using troughs to catch the sap, but soon had the best pine buckets, which he made himself. He boiled the sap in a three-barrel kettle, made more than an inch thick, and shaped liked an earthen bowl, it having ears on the sides by which it was hung over the fire. When the fire was in full blaze the sap would boil furiously, but a slice of pork thrown into it would prevent its running over. If this sugar was not as nice as our modern sugar it was sweet and palatable, even if it had been strained in order to get the coals and leaves out of it, and everybody was invited to try it in the sugaring time. Capt. Stone was skilled in manufacturing salts for market. He would cut and pile the maple and birch, then burn it and collect the ashes, obtain lye, boil it and run it into casks or kettles to harden. On one occasion he had a five-pail kettle of salts that had hardened, and in trying to split the salts, for which he used an iron wedge, he split the salts and the kettle as well. Mr. Stone held many town offices, and in 1823 was captain of a militia company. He sold the farm and moved to the mill, occupying the house that J. P. Long now owns, but emigrated to Ohio in 1837, where he and wife died soon after. Benjamin Stiles owned and lived on this place until 1839, when he sold it to F. P. Batchelder, who sold it to Zachariah Whitney. He lived on the farm until 1854, when he sold it to F. B. Smith, who sold it to the Stone brothers, the present owners.

CHILDREN OF JOSIAH STONE.

Mary died in May, 1827, aged 16 years.

Josiah died in May, 1827, aged 14 years.

Eunice went to Ohio, married there; now dead.

Susan went to Ohio, married there; now dead.

Martha went to Ohio, married, now lives in Peru.

Ezra went to Ohio, married; died in 1881.

John Batchelder began new on the farm now occupied by his son, Deacon Edmund Batchelder. He built the first framed house east from present house in 1805, cleared up the land and built the wall. In 1823 he built the present house and moved into it, his son Edmund taking the old house. The farm has been in the hands of father, son and grandson for ninety years, and is now in the possession of Edmund Batchelder and his son Hildreth. Improvements have recently been made on the house, and two new barns, which are the best in town, have been built.

CHILDREN OF DEACON JOHN BATCHELDER.

Mark m. Roxby Conant of Grafton, lived in Peru; died in 1863, aged 60 years.

Fanny m. Lawrence McMullen, died in New York State in 1835, aged 30 years.

Eliza m. Rev. Benjamin Springer, lived in New York State, moved to Ohio; died in 1846.

John died at Peru in 1822, aged 13 years and 7 months.

Edmund m. Sophia Simonds, who died October 27th, 1856, aged 41 years.

Mary m. David Parker of Derry, lives there.

Mahala m. Thomas Manley of Dorset for her first husband, and Clinton Lord of Putney for her second; she died in 1865.

Josiah died in infancy.

CHILDREN OF DEACON EDMUND BATCHELDER.

Harlan m. Elsie Lakin, died at Peru in 1868, aged 30 years.

Martha died young.

Clark m. Josie Hard, lives in Ayer Junction, Mass.

Newton m. Jennie Burnham, lives in Newfane.

Hildreth m. Ida Davis, lives in Peru.

There was another son that died young.

Joseph Dodge came from Amherst, N. H., in 1804, and began on the farm now owned by Charles Batchelder. He built part of the house and cleared some of the land, remaining there until 1818, when he sold out to Edmund Batchelder and moved to Manchester, afterwards going to New York State, where he died. Edmund Batchelder came from Mt. Vernon, N. H., in 1819, and erected all the buildings now on the place, also cleared and improved the farm until he had over 300 acres of good land. He died on the farm in July, 1869, aged 83 years, and his wife died the same month, aged 85 years. Charles Batchelder, Edmund's son, now owns the place.

CHILDREN OF EDMUND BATCHELDER.

Ira K. m. Nancy Barnard, lived in Peru, moved to Townshend.

Francis P. m. Abigail Barnard, lived in Peru until 1869, then moved to Ludlow, afterwards to Iowa, now living in Dakota.

Roxana m. Jonas Dale of Weston, moved to Jamaica, where he died in 1845, and she then married William L. Waterman; she died at Derry in November, 1868.

Amos m. Lucretia Jones of Waitsfield, lives in Peru.

Daniel m. Betsey Utley of Landgrove, lived in South Derry; died in 1886.

Hannah m. G. S. Hobart of Derry, died in 1870.

Charles m. Abbie Davis, lives in Peru.

James died October 24th, 1835, aged 6 years.

CHILDREN OF CHARLES BATCHELDER.

Charles K. m., lives in Beaufort, S. C.

Frank m., lives in Boston.

Nellie m. Robert I. Batchelder, lives in Peru.

Mark, unmarried, lives in Beaufort, S. C.

Edna lives with her parents.

Kittridge Mather began new on the farm where he lived in 1830, and erected the buildings and cleared the land, living on the place for more than 40 years. He was married twice. Mr. Mather died in 1883.

Levi Batchelder commenced on the farm north of Charles Batchelder's in 1829, clearing the land and building a frame house. He was an active, industrious man, and did a good deal of work for other people besides looking after his own farm. He was a useful member of the Methodist church, and led a good, Christian life. Mr. Batchelder lived an active life almost to the time of his death, which occurred in 1856, at the age of 60 years. After his

MRS. AARON BEARD.

AARON BEARD.

death the farm was run by F. B. Smith, his son-in-law, and Mrs. Batchelder, who lived with him until she died.

CHILDREN OF LEVI BATCHELDER.

Mary M. John Gregg of New Boston, N. H., lived and died there.

Eben C. M. Miss Kittridge of Mt. Vernon, N. H., lives in Milford, N. H.

Belinda M. John Hart, lived in New Hampshire; died in Peru in 1873, aged 53 years.

Betsey M. William Davis, lives in Weston, Vt.

Ann M. F. B. Smith, lived on the homestead; died in 1888.

Noah M. in Amherst, N. H., lives in Lowell, Mass.

Levi, unmarried, lived in Peru; died in November, 1885.

Sarah M. T. J Lakin, died at Landgrove in 1882.

Fanny M. A. P. D. Simonds, lived in Peru; he was killed with a mower. Fanny then married Clark Bryant, lives in Peru.

CHILDREN OF F. P. BATCHELDER.

Rosette M. J. L. Israel, lives in St. Louis.

Mary Emma M. Mr. Stewart, lives in Colorado.

Luella M. Mr. Knight, lives in St. Louis.

Herbert M. in Iowa, lives there.

Lizza M. Mr. Crank, lives in Iowa.

The lot on which J. P. Long resides was began by Isaac Bigelow, one of the early settlers, who built a log house and barn on the right of the road, and in the corner of the lot. In 1819 he sold the farm to Joseph Stone and moved to Pawlet, John H. Dudley using the log house for a schoolhouse. Joseph Stone put up the frame of the present house in 1825, covered the outside, and sold the place to Josiah Stone, who finished the house and lived in it until 1837, when he sold out to Oliver Wyman, he buying the mill at the same time. Isaac G. Long bought the farm and mill a year or two later, and, with the help of his son, carried on the farm, they also improved the mill by repairing the dam and putting in turning works. The mill was kept running until Mr. Long's death in 1850, when his sons sold it, with the land connected with it, to Holland Tarble. J. P. Long has made great improvements in the farm, and has erected some good buildings.

CHILDREN OF ISAAC G. LONG.

Remembrance M. James Farnum, lived in Peru; died in 1886.

Joseph P. M. Elvira Lakin, she died in Peru in 1859; he then married Widow Oliver Lincoln, lived in Peru. Joseph died in 1885.

Charles m. Martha Batchelder, lived in Detroit, Mich.; she died in 1889, and was interred at Manchester.

Mary m. Elijah Carlton, lives in 'Derry.

CHILDREN OF J. P. LONG.

Madison enlisted in the army during the war, was sent to Brattleboro, where he was taken sick, never fully recovering. He died in 1866.

One son died young.

Henry m, lived in Peru, moved to Manchester.

Francis Bennett came from Groton, Mass., in 1819, and began on the lot east of Edmund Batchelder's farm, living on the Atkins place until 1821, when he had a comfortable log house to move into. The land was covered with maple, birch, beech, hemlock, spruce and balsam, which, with the help of his boys, Mr. Bennett cut down, soon having a good farm. He cultivated hops for several years and made it pay, but finding that they spoilt the soil he gave it up and used the land for other purposes. Mr. Bennett held several town offices, and was a prominent and useful member of the Methodist church. After he had put up all the buildings that are now on the farm he sold out to S. W. Lincoln, and lived on various farms in town until he moved to Troy, N. Y., from which place he went to Salem, Mass., where he died in 1868. He had moved more times than any other man in town, and a neighbor, "Uncle Fred," once asked him if he would be contented when he got to Heaven. There were nine children in the family.

CHILDREN OF FRANCIS BENNETT.

Francis enlisted in the army in 1825 and went to St. Paul, but returned for a short time, when he went away and roamed over the country until his death.

Lucinda m. Joseph Barnard, but did not live with him long; she married again and went to New York State.

Jacob was a merchant in New York, died of cholera in 1831.

James married a lady from Boston, lived in Peru and Rockingham, afterwards went into business with his son in Boston.

William went to sea and was never heard of since.

Thomas married in Green Bay, Mich., lived there.

Rufus married and went to Michigan; now keeps a hotel.

Samuel died at Peru in 1839.

George went South in 1842.

Caroline m. Mr. Davis of Rockingham, moved West.

Deacon John Davidson came from Plymouth, Vt., in 1837, and bought his farm from S. W. Lincoln. He was quite advanced in years when he came to town, some of his children being at that time settled in different places, while some came with him. Deacon Davidson represented the town two years in the legislature. He helped to build the church and parsonage, and was always ready to help support any good cause by his means and presence. On his eighty-fourth birthday he rode two miles on horseback to attend the weekly prayer meeting, saying that it was his eighty-fourth birthday and he had lived to enjoy twelve years of Sabbaths; this was the last meeting he attended. He died on December 28th, 1858, aged 84 years. After his death the farm was carried on by his son-in-law, Harley Coolidge, who died in 1889, leaving the farm to his son John, the present occupant.

CHILDREN OF DEACON JOHN DAVIDSON.

Lydia m. Daniel Coolidge, lives in Ludlow.

Sarepta, unmarried, died at Peru in 1872.

Clarissa m. Harley Coolidge, died at Peru in 1875, aged 64 years.

Sarah and Mary died in Peru when young.

Daniel went to Illinois about 1845, married there.

Flavel died when a young man in Peru.

CHILDREN OF HARLEY COOLIDGE.

Chalmers m. Nellie Wise, he is a clergyman in Fairfield, Vt.

Sarah m. Romaine Spaulding, lives in Weston.

Mary Emma m. Job Scott, lives in Weston.

John m. Ina Smith, lives in Peru.

Nathaniel Russell came from Jamaica in the autumn of 1838, and settled on the farm where Burkett Simonds lives, where he stayed five years, selling out to F. P. Batchelder. In 1844 he and his son bought the place where M. J. Walker lives, and lived on it twelve years, when Mr. Russell sold his share to Samuel and bought the Silas Staples farm in company with his son, O. N. Russell. They rebuilt the barns and improved the house, also made great improvements in the farm, but sold the place in 1867 to J. G. Batchelder and moved to Arlington, where Mr. Russell died in 1870, aged 74 years. Mrs. Betsey Russell, his wife, died at Deacon Batchelder's residence at Peru in 1879, aged 76 years.

CHILDREN OF NATHANIEL RUSSELL.

Samuel B. m. Hannah Lawrence, lived on his farm in Peru some years and then moved to Landgrove, where he still lives.

Philetus H. м. Mary Wyman, lived on the Ira Wait farm, the Joel Adams farm, and on the Jackson farm, but afterwards moved to Arlington, where his wife died. Laurin, his only son, enlisted in the army in 1863 and was killed in the war. Philetus now resides in Michigan.

Ziba м. Sarah Robbins, enlisted in the army from Lawrence, Mass., and was killed in the war.

Lysander м. Mary Simonds, lives in Natick, Mass.

Obadiah N. м. Janett Walker, she died at Peru in 1863, aged 22 years. Obadiah enlisted in the army at the time of the war, and after his discharge married Sarah Ann (Simonds) Quackenbush. He died at Arlington in 1867.

Joseph G. Whitney came from Westminster, Mass., in 1805, and began new on the lot where Clark Lakin lives, putting up the first buildings on the place. Soon after he settled his father came to see him, was taken sick in the house with typhus fever and died, he being one of the first that was buried in the north cemetery. Mr. Whitney was a useful man, both to the town and to society. About 1814 he sold the farm to Capt. James Lincoln and moved to Westminster. Capt. Lincoln kept the farm two or three years, selling out to Norman Whitney, who came to town with his father, Elisha Whitney, Norman having worked several years for Gov. Skinner in Manchester. He married Belinda Batchelder of Landgrove, and lived on the farm until 1827, when he sold out to James Lakin and moved to Andover, from there to Chester, and then to Putney, where they both died, leaving one daughter, who is still living there. Mr. Lakin built the present house and improved the barns, living there until he died in 1875, aged 68 years, when his son Clark continued to carry on the farm.

CHILDREN OF JAMES LAKIN.

Laura died at Peru in 1850, aged 19 years.

Susan died at Lowell in 1859, aged 25 years.

Harriet died in Massachusetts.

Jane м. W. H. Eddy of Winhall, lives in Townshend.

Clark R. м. Elvira Rideout of Dorset, lives on the homestead in Peru.

Anna м. E. B. Batchelder, lives in Townshend.

Elsa м. Harlan Batchelder for her first husband, and Elliot Morse for her second.

Addie м. S. E. Garfield, lives in Townshend.

JESSE WARREN

The farm on which Rocius Fairbanks lives was a pitched lot, made by Asa Hull, and was under the jurisdiction of Landgrove until the present jurisdictional line was made and established in 1836 or '37, when it became part of Peru. Mr. Hull built the buildings in 818, but sold out to Nathaniel Richardson, who sold it to his son Ralph. Ezra Dodge bought the place from him in 1839 and lived on it about ten years, when he sold out to William Davis, who occupied it a few years. He sold the place to Zimri Lathrop, who was burnt out while living there, but, with the help of the citizens, he built another house, living in it several years. T. J. Lakin next bought the place, and lived on it a few years, when he sold out to Mr. Ballard, who sold it to George Richardson, he selling it to Sarah Russell. Rocius Fairbanks then bought the place and lived on it until 1889, when he sold out to George Richardson, who is the present owner.

There was a lot north of the Hull farm know as Mather's clearing, with a log house, a barn, and a large apple tree on it. The place can be remembered as far back as 1820, but nothing is known of the person who built and cleared the place. It is now owned by John Coolidge.

The place east of the Mather lot was began by Mr. Scripture, who sold it to Jonathan Bruce. He erected comfortable buildings and had a very good farm, but after his death it was deserted. The place is now owned by R. Fairbanks, who has removed all the old buildings.

The farm east of John Coolidge's was commenced by Jacob Bennett, a brother to Francis Bennett, about 1825, and who built a log house and cleared some of the land. After living on the place a few years he sold it to James Farnum, who improved it and then sold out to Martin Granger. He lived there a while and sold the place to Charles Farnum, he selling it to Charles W. Jenkins, who improved the buildings and land very much. Mr. Jenkins died on this farm April 17, 1883, aged 43 years. Charles Moffat is the present owner and occupant.

The farm on which Burkitt Simonds lives was bought from Peter Allen by Joel Adams, Jr., about 1825, it being then in its natural state. Mr. Adams cleared some of the land and built a house and barn, remaining on the place until 1839, when he sold out to N. Russell. About four years later F. P. Batchelder bought it, but did not live on the place. Freeman Lyon and G. W. Carlton both lived on this farm before Asa Simonds bought and occupied it, William Simonds came into possession of the place, and made great improvements in the buildings and land.

Dana Wyman built the house on the lot east of W. B. Simonds's farm, and it has been occupied by Freeman Lyon, Allen Benson and Nahum Russell. Joseph and Albert Simonds bought it as an addition to their farm.

Joel Nason began on a lot south of A. T. Byard's farm, but sold out to Jesse Lanphere, who cleared the land and built a house. He was hurt by a horse while working on the farm and never fully recovered. Duane Walker was the next one that lived on the farm, and died there about 1855, when James H. Wait bought it. This place was in charge of P. T. Wyman for some time.

The farm that is now owned by A. T. Byard was begun in 1835 by Asa Phillips, who built a log house and barn and cleared the land. He afterwards erected a frame house and barn, and sold out to J. H. Simonds, who made some additions to the buildings. P. D. Wyman next bought the farm and lived on it several years, selling out to A. T. Byard, the present owner.

Josiah Brown came from Princeton, Mass., in 1803, and built a house on the old road that runs from M. B. Lyon's house, through the Whitney lot, to Deacon Wyman's old house, and not far from Deacon Seth Lyon's house. Mr. Brown lived on this place several years and then returned to Manchester, no one ever living on the place since.

George W. Whitcomb built a house where F. Lyon now lives, and occupied it until about 1822, when he left town, selling the place to Thomas Wyman, who lived there a year or two. Anna Lawrence next owned the place, and afterwards Thomas Lawrence, he occupying it for nearly thirty years. He died at the house of his son-in-law, S. B. Russell. N Russell occupied this place a year or two, then sold it to Charles Farnum, who sold out to Nathan Lillie. The present owner and occupant is Freeman Lyon.

The schoolhouse near Freeman Lyon's house was built in 1831, and a summer school was kept in it when it was only boarded up on the outside, but was finished before the winter school commenced. All the children from the village, the Lyon, Bigelow and Holton farms went there to school. This house was used as a schoolhouse about fifty years, when the one east of it was built.

Landen Jenkins built his house and barn near the Haynes mill

n 1870; he also erected a blacksmith shop, in which he has since
worked at his trade.

Henry Long built a house on the opposite side of the road from
Mr. Jenkins's place, and lived in it a short time. It has been
occupied by several families since he moved out.

Asa Bailey lived on the place west of the Hapgood farm for a
short time. Mr. Hutchins next occupied the place, and built a shop
on the brook near the schoolhouse, where he manufactured chairs,
using water power to cut and turn his stock. He left town about
1822, John Chandler and Parker Wyman buying the place and
manufacturing rakes there. Isaac G. Long next bought the place,
and lived on it until 1838, when he sold out to Oliver Wyman, who
occupied it several years. He sold the place to William Whitney,
and it was he that built the present house, but lived there only a
few years, selling out to Zimri Whitney. Mr. Whitney lived on the
farm until he died, when his daughter, Mrs. Penfield, came into
possession of it. Joseph Hapgood, A. C. Sloan, Freeman Lyon, and
several others have lived on this farm. It was owned by Nathan
Lillie a short time, but he never occupied it.

The house at the fork of the road on the way to the Burt farm
was built by Eliab Stone. Asa Phillips, Jr., and Dana Wyman both
lived on this place. John Q. Adams bought it and built a barn, but
did not keep it long.

Capt. William Utley came from Connecticut in 1769, cutting his
road from Chester to Bromley, and settled on the farm now owned by
Menzie Thompson, the place still being known as the Utley flats.
He attended two of the first conventions of New Hampshire Grants
as delegate from Bromley. He soon found that there was a gore of
land west of Andover and 'Derry, and east of Bromley, not included
in the charter of any town, and he, with others, obtained a charter of
the gore from the government of Vermont. They proceeded to
survey the gore and establish a western line between the town of
Bromley and the gore, but the proprietors of Bromley did not
acquiesce in Utley's western line. He remained on his land, but did
not attend any more conventions as a delegate from Bromley.

William Barlow came to town in 1773 and settled on the farm
where M. B. Lyon resides. He built his house near a spring on the
lower side of the road, not far from the present house. It is
supposed that he died in town and was buried in the south-west
corner of the Holton farm. It is not known as he had any family,
probably not.

Asa Farnum and wife came to town in 1811 and settled in school district No. 6, building a log house on the land now owned by Luther M. Tuttle. His house was built without any chimney, having a hole in the roof to let the smoke out, and his only floor was the bare ground. He did not stay in town many years, but went to live with his son-in-law, Grovnenr Davis, where he died in 1861, aged 82 years. Mr. Farnum was a soldier in the war of 1812.

About 1803 Deacon John Batchelder cleared a piece of land on the lot now owned by the heirs of Joseph Utley, which he used as a pasture until he sold it to Stephen Tuttle and his son, E. H. Tuttle, who built a house on it. This was in 1826, and was the first permanent settlement in district No. 6. Stephen Tuttle died on this farm on November 23, 1851, and his wife died on October 20, 1851. E. H. Tuttle sold his interest in the farm to his brother, Stephen Tuttle, who married Rebecca Lampson. Stephen died on the farm of typhus fever on October 5, 1850, aged 56 years, leaving five children, namely: Cyrus, who died in Andersonville prison, James, Lucinda, Sophronia and Norman. The next one that owned the farm was George Pease, he selling out to Joseph R. Utley, who died on the farm on November 3, 1881. His only daughter married Merritt Cook, who now lives on the farm with the widow of Joseph R. Utley.

Reuben Lampson's farm was began by E. H. Tuttle and Moses Leonard, who sold out to Joseph Holt. He sold the farm to Ebenezer H. Lampson, who came from Weston. Both Mr. and Mrs. Lampson died on the place, the place going into the hands of their son Reuben. He married Miranda Woodward for his first wife, and Widow Diantha (Cook) Whitney for his second. There were six children by the first wife and two by the second. Reuben and his son Rodney now live on the farm.

CHILDREN OF REUBEN LAMPSON.

Wallace M. Miss Smith, lives in Manchester.

Rodney M. Katie Whitney, lives in Peru.

Amasa, Lewis, Geary and Elmer.

After E. H. Tuttle sold the Lampson farm he went out of town. His wife died in Grafton on October 26, 1839, and he then married Hannah Felton, who died in 1880, aged 71 years. On his return to Peru he lived on the farm now occupied by his son, Luther M. Tuttle. Mr. Tuttle built a mill on this place about 1842, and occupied it until 1850, when he sold it, with one acre of land, to

MRS. J. L. HAYNES.

J. L. HAYNES.

Moses Smiley.   Mr. Tuttle died on this farm on June 9, 1875, aged 75 years.

Malvina, Keziah, Rosette, William E., Sarah, Amanda, Charles W., Warren C., George, Betsey, Miranda, Abby, Lucy, Emma, Irene, and Luther M

Mr. Smiley erected a house on the piece of land sold to him by E. H. Tuttle, and then sold the place to Hiram Davis, who sold out to William E. and Warren C. Tuttle.   E. H. Tuttle purchased the place of them and sold it to Edward Burnap, he selling it back again to Mr. Tuttle, who then sold to Warren C. Tuttle.   He sold it to the present owner, Oscar J. Esterbrook.

James Wait came from Weston, Vt., in 1835, and settled on the present Wait farm.   He cleared a small piece of land and soon had a comfortable house built on it.   In the fall of 1835 he returned to Weston, but came back again the next year, when he cleared his land and erected a saw mill, giving energy and thrift to the whole school district.   School was kept in his house until 1839, when a schoolhouse was built.   Esquire Wait was a strong, muscular man, and very energetic in all his movements to carry out his plans, whether of a public or a private nature.   He was a strong Democrat, and held town offices at different times.   Mr. Wait died on the farm on March 10, 1854, and his widow then went to live with her son Albert, where she died in 1879.

James H. M. Nancy L. Wyman, lives in East Dorset.

Nelson M. Jane Miles of Weston, died in Weston.

Albert M. Sarah Davis of Londonderry, lived on the homestead several years, moved to East Dorset; died there in 1877.

Lucretia, died young at Peru in 1844.

The lot north of the Wait farm was begun by Hiram Barney and Roswell Rowell about 1832, but they sold the place to John S. Rumrill, who sold it to William Strong.   It is now owned by the Stone brothers. There is no building on this lot.

The lot west of the Barney place was begun by Thomas K. Hall, who was killed soon after he commenced work on the place by a tree falling on him.   Royal Bryant owned this place a short time, but sold it to Martin Granger, who lived on it several years, then selling out to George Emerson, he being the last occupant.   It is now owned by the Stone brothers.

The Grovneur Davis farm was begun by Isham Purdy about 1827, who built a frame house and barn and lived on the place several years. He sold it to Mr. Thrasher in 1833, an l he sold it to G. Davis, who improved the farm and erected new buildings, living on it 40 years. He moved to Landgrove in 1882, and lived with his son in-law until he died in 1884. Mrs. Davis is still living. Robert, Mr. Davis's son, now occupies the farm.

CHILDREN OF GROVNEUR DAVIS.

Betsey Nancy m. Daniel Eddy.

John m. Amanda Roby, lives in Manchester.

Henry m., keeps a hotel at Factory Point.

Ann m. Myron Piper.

Robert m. Josephine Nichols.

Sumner Wait began on a lot north of the G. Davis place about 1832, and lived there a short time, selling out to Mr. Kingsbury, who lived on it for a time. It has not been occupied since.

It has been impossible to find out who built the house in which Herbert C. Woodward now lives. It has been owned and occupied by the following: Wellman Hale, E. H. Tuttle, Amos Jenkins, William Camp, William E. Tuttle, Jefferson French, John Davis, and H. C. Woodward.

ROADS.

The first highway laid out in Bromley was in 1787, on the west side of the mountain, (now in Dorset). The committee who laid it was Aaron Dewey and Mr. Byrns, with Jonathan Aikin as surveyor.

The first road laid on the east side of the mountain was in June, 1797, by a committee appointed by the legislature at a session held in 1788, consisting of George Sexton and Asa Utley. They were empowered to lay a public road through the town, and expend a tax of two cents, granted by said legislature, on each acre of land in said town for making roads and building bridges. The road laid by said committee commenced 3½ miles and 40 rods north from the south-east corner of the town in the east line of the town, thence running westerly and south-west by Charles and Edmund Batchelder's place below the stone mill, up the Stratton hill by David Stratton's house, across the Chandler brook, where it does at this time, thence back of the house occupied by Nathan Lillie, also on the hill back of M. G. Walker's house, thence runs on the west of the orchard and brick and on the Deacon Wyman farm, by the old mill near I. R.

Walker's, by the Gen. Dudley buildings, through the Benjamin Barnard farm, by the Butterfield tavern on top of the mountain, thence westerly down the mountain, through Peru and Winhall to Manchester. This road ran in Peru 6 miles and 94 rods. In 1800 this road, from the Chandler brook by Esquire Bigelow's, was altered to its present location. This was the main traveled road across the mountain until the turnpike was built in 1816, on which the travel has been to the present time.

In 1799 the legislature granted another land tax of three cents per acre for making roads and bridges. The committee appointed to lay out roads and expend the money were Jonathan Butterfield and Aaron Killam.

The second road laid commenced at the south-east corner of M. G. Walker's farm, thence west on a line between 4th and 5th ranges of lots, 212 rods to the Holt place, known as the Moss farm. Also a road from David Stratton's, running west thirty-five degrees, north 223 rods, to Isaac Jackson's house. Also another road commencing at the south corner of Reuben Bigelow's land, running east, then south by Aaron Killam's house to Benjamin Barnard's (Sen.) place. Also laid a road from Aaron Killam's to Landgrove line. This road was laid on the brook through the burnt meadow. Also in 1801 a road was laid from the great road, commencing at a stone standing half-way between the houses of Deacon Seth Lyon and Josiah Brown, (these houses stood on W. W. Whitney's land), thence east and south by the cellar hole in G. K. Davis's garden to the Bryant shop, east of the line between the Hapgood place and M. B. Lyon's pasture, running by the Burt house to the William Pollard house. Jonathan Butterfield and Aaron Killam were appointed to lay out and make these roads, which were made by the land tax granted in 1799, expended by the above committee.

After this time the roads were laid by the selectmen and made by the inhabitants of the town. The main roads have been well built and kept in good repair, but the back roads are not so good.

In 1814 the legislature granted a charter for the Peru turnpike, commencing near the Lovell farm, running westerly five miles towards Manchester village to the east line of Manchester. It was laid out and built as it is now, with the exception of a short piece in Winhall, by the spot where the Chapin mill stood, which has been altered. Three-fourths of this road is in Winhall. Work was commenced on it in 1815, and was finished in 1816. Gen. Peter Dudley had the job of building the road, and worked on it repairing for more than twenty years, keeping it in excellent condition. A great amount of teaming and travel was done on the road until 1850, when the railroads diverted the travel to other places. At the time that it was built it was convenient to all towns east of it to the Connecticut river. The travel from Boston to Saratoga and west crossed the mountain here.

In 1820 commissioners were appointed by the Supreme Court to lay a road and alter the stage road from Chester to the east end of the Peru turnpike. The alterations made in Peru began at the place where Freeman Lyon now lives, by laying a new road westerly to the place where Everett Adams lives. The old road ran by the Holton farm to the road running north and south from M. B Lyon's house, back of John Adams's house, south-west of the wall that divides W. W. Whitney's land from land belonging to the hotel lot to the Wyman place, where it was discontinued. A road was made from M. B. Lyon's house to the tavern house in 1821.

In 1849 and '50 Ira Cochran erected the notch mill, coming up the Mad Tom on the west side of the mountain. He petitioned for a road across the mountain to Peru. The first committee laid the road from Dorset to the mill, the town paying for it. A subsequent committee laid the road over the mountain to Peru in 1871, and is of use to the north part of the town and Landgrove. It made a heavy tax on the town, and is a bill of expense to keep it in repair.

The early or first roads made in Peru were built with money raised by land tax granted by the legislature on all the land in town, and expended by a committee appointed by them. The last land tax granted was about 1823, and amounted to three cents per acre, the committee appointed to expend the money being Capt. James Lincoln and Parker Wyman.

HON. DEXTER BATCHELDER

appoint officers to govern 3d. town as the law directs. Meeting duly warned and signed. Joseph Curtis, Justice of the Peace. Bromley, March 2nd, 1802.

The inhabitants met, agreeable to notice, in the dwelling of E. Hurlburt, and chose John Brock, town clerk; David White, Aaron Killam, and Ebenezer Hurlburt, selectmen; John Brock and Jonathan Butterfield, listers; Reuben Bigelow and David Colson, constables. Attested by John Brock, town clerk.

The next town meeting was appointed to be held at the Butter-field Inn, on the height of land between Manchester and Peru. The people on the west side of the mountain demurred, but attended the first meeting held there, after which they petitioned to be set to Dorset, but Dorset would not receive them. They then applied to Mt. Tabor, which received them, and a tract of land two hundred rods wide and six miles long was set to Mt. Tabor, and received the cognomen of Mt. Tabor Leg. This piece of land was afterwards set to Dorset.

TOWN OFFICERS.

SELECTMEN.

1802. David White, Aaron Killam, Ebenezer Hurlburt.
1803. Moses Hill, John Brock, Thomas Wyman.
1804. Reuben Bigelow, Thomas Wyman, John Brock.
1805. Reuben Bigelow, Samuel Cooper, Elias Beebe.
1806. Aaron Killam, Seth Lyon, Elijah Simonds.
1807. Joseph Fairbank, Peter Dudley, Jeduthan Bruce.
1808. Joseph Fairbank, Peter Dudley, Jeduthan Bruce.
1809. Joseph Fairbank, Peter Dudley, Jeduthan Bruce.
1810. Joseph Fairbank, Peter Dudley, Jeduthan Bruce.
1811. Joseph Fairbank, Thomas Wyman. John Batchelder.
1812. Reuben Bigelow, Thomas Wyman, John Batchelder.
1813. John Batchelder, Elijah Simonds, Israel Batchelder.
1814. John Batchelder, Elijah Simonds, Israel Batchelder.
1815. Reuben Bigelow, John Batchelder, Elijah Simonds.
1816. Reuben Bigelow, John Batchelder, Elijah Simonds.
1817. Reuben Bigelow, Elijah Simonds, Samuel Stone.
1818. Reuben Bigelow, Samuel Stone, Josiah Barnard.
1819. Reuben Bigelow, Samuel Stone, Josiah Barnard.
1820. Reuben Bigelow, Samuel Stone, Seth Lyon.
1821. Peter Dudley, Samuel Stone, Seth Lyon.

1822. Peter Dudley, Samuel Stone, Josiah Barnard.
1823. Josiah Barnard, Thomas Wyman, Seth Lyon.
1824. Josiah Stone, Seth Lyon, Thomas Wyman.
1825. Seth Lyon, Israel Batchelder, Josiah Hapgood.
1826. Seth Lyon, Israel Batchelder, Josiah Hapgood
1827. Daniel Tuthill, Peter Dudley, Edmund Batchelder.
1828. Peter Dudley, Edmund Batchelder, Benjamin Barnard, Jr.
1829. Peter Dudley, Edmund Batchelder, Benjamin Barnard.
1830. Benjamin Barnard, Edmund Batchelder, Francis Bennett.
1831. Benjamin Barnard, Edmund Batchelder, Francis Bennett.
1832. Benjamin Barnard, Reuben Bigelow, Peter Dudley.
1833. Benjamin Barnard, Reuben Bigelow, Peter Dudley.
1834. Benjamin Barnard, Jr., Peter Dudley, James Lincoln.
1835. Benjamin Barnard, Peter Dudley, James Lincoln.
1836. Peter Dudley, Nathan Whitney, Stillman W. Lincoln.
1837. Israel Batchelder, Jonas B. Bennett, Amherst Messenger.
1838. Jonas B. Bennett, Amherst Messenger, Jonathan R. Wyman.
1839. Benjamin Barnard, Francis Bennett, J. J. Hapgood.
1840. Benjamin Barnard, Aaron Burton, Joel Lyon.
1841. Benjamin Barnard, Joel Lyon, Freeman Lyon.
1842. Benjamin Barnard, Aaron Burton, Ezra Dodge.
1843. James Wait, Benjamin S. Ballard, Ezra Dodge.
1844. James Wait, Benjamin S. Ballard, Ira K. Batchelder.
1845. Ira K. Batchelder, Ezra Dodge, George Batchelder.
1846. George Batchelder, Stephen Dudley, Cephas Bailey.
1847. George Batchelder, Stephen Dudley, Cephas Bailey.
1848. Jesse Rider, Mark Batchelder, Z. F. Whitney.
1849. Jesse Rider, Aaron Burton, Z. F. Whitney.
1850. Jesse Rider, Edward Batchelder, Stephen Dudley.
1851. Jesse Rider, Edward Batchelder, Stephen Dudley.
1852. Edward Batchelder, Aaron Burton, Mark Batchelder.
1853. Aaron Burton, Mark Batchelder, Stephen Dudley.
1854. Aaron Burton, Mark Batchelder, Stephen Dudley.
1855. Z. F. Whitney, J. G. Mellendy, Cephas Bailey.
1856. Ira K. Batchelder, Joseph Long, Jonathan Hapgood.
1857. Ira K. Batchelder, J. P. Long, Jonathan Hapgood.
1858. Ira K. Batchelder, Dexter Batchelder, John G. Mellendy.
1859. Ira K. Batchelder, Dexter Batchelder, Jonathan Hapgood.
1860. Ira K. Batchelder, Dexter Batchelder, Jonathan Hapgood.
1861. Ira K. Batchelder, Harvey Stone, Stephen D. Simonds.

1862. Ira K. Batchelder, Harvey Stone, Stephen D. Simonds.
1863. Ira K. Batchelder, Jonathan Hapgood, Ira R. Walker.
1864. Ira K. Batchelder, Jonathan Hapgood, Ira R. Walker.
1865. Ira K. Batchelder, Jonathan Hapgood, Ira R. Walker.
1866. Ira K. Batchelder, Jonathan Hapgood, Ira R. Walker.
1867. Jonathan Hapgood, Ira R. Walker, G. K. Davis.
1868. Ira R. Walker, G. K. Davis, J. H. Simonds.
1869. Jonathan Hapgood, J. P. Long, Harvey Stone.
1870. Jonathan Hapgood, Harvey Stone, J. P. Long.
1871. Jonathan Hapgood, Harvey Stone, J. P. Long.
1872. Harvey Stone, A. C. Nourse, John G. Walker.
1873. A. C. Nourse, John G. Walker, Charles Batchelder.
1874. A. C. Nourse, A. H. Williams, Samuel Stiles.
1875. Harvey Stone, Jonathan Hapgood, James C. Lakin.
1876. Harvey Stone, Jonathan Hapgood, James C. Lakin.
1877. John G. Walker, M. B. Lyon, E. R. Hart.
1878. John G. Walker, M. B. Lyon, E. R. Hart.
1879. E. R. Hart, Samuel Stiles, A. H. Williams.
1880. Samuel Stiles, A. H. Williams, G. K. Davis.
1881. J. G. Walker, G. K. Davis, J. C. Lakin.
1882. J. G. Walker, G. K. Davis, W. B. Simonds.
1883. J. G. Walker, W. B. Simonds, M. B. Lyon.
1884. J. G. Walker, M. B. Lyon, J. C. Lakin.
1885. J. G. Walker, M. B. Lyon, J. C. Lakin.
1886. J. G. Walker, M. B. Lyon, J. C. Lakin.
1887. J. C. Lakin, R. I. Batchelder, W. J. Farnum.
1888. R. I. Batchelder, W. J. Farnum, Samuel Stiles.

TOWN CLERKS.

John Brook, 1802.
William Pollard, 1803 to 1807.
Joseph Fairbank, 1807 to 1812.
Reuben Bigelow, 1812 to 1835.
Russell Tuthill, 1835 to 1837.
Israel Batchelder, 1837 to 1839.
Thomas Baldwin, 1839 to 1845.
Ira K. Batchelder, 1845 to 1852.
O. P. Simonds, 1852 to 1869.
Charles W. Whitney, 1869 to 1873.
O. P. Simonds, 1873 to 1889.

CONSTABLES.

Aaron Killam, 1803 to 1812.
Seth Lyon, 1804 to 1805.
Joseph Fairbank, 1805 to 1810.
Mendal Fosgate, 1807 to 1809.
Silas Clark, 1808 to 1809.
Josiah Barnard, 1812 to 1818.
Asa Simonds, 1818 to 1821.
Nathan Whitney, 1821 to 1828.
Peter Dudley, 1828 to 1829.
Nathan Whitney, 1829 to 1836.
Mark Batchelder, 1836 to 1838.
George Batchelder, 1838 to 1840.
Stephen Dudley, 1840 to 1843.
Freeman Lyon, 1843 to 1846.
George Batchelder, 1846 to 1847.
F. P. Batchelder, 1847 to 1860.
J. H. Simonds, 1860 to 1861.
James Lincoln, 1861 to 1864.
P. J. Walker, 1864 to 1868.
M. B. Lyon, 1868 to 1869.
Wesley Woodward, 1869 to 1870.
James Lincoln, 1870 to 1872.
George K. Davis, 1872 to 1880.
J. B. Simonds, 1880 to 1883.
M. G. Walker, 1883 to 1885.
George K. Davis, 1885 to 1890.

JUSTICES OF THE PEACE.

Reuben Bigelow, Peter Dudley, Israel Batchelder, Samuel Stone, Daniel Tuthill, Josiah Barnard, Seth Lyon, Sen., James Wait, Amherst Messenger, J. G. Walker, M. B. Lyon, J. C. Lakin, A. C. Nourse, Ira R. Walker, C. M. Russell, Freeman Lyon, B. S. Ballard, I. K. Batchelder, James Lincoln, E. H. Tuttle, Stephen Dudley, J. H. Simonds, F. K. Stiles, J. P. Long, Jonathan Hapgood, J. R. Utley, M. J. Hapgood, E. R. Hart, J Chadwick.

MEMBERS OF LEGISLATURE.

Reuben Bigelow, 1803, 1804, 1805, 1828.
Peter Dudley, 1808, 1809, 1810, 1812, 1814, 1816, 1818, 1832, 1833.

Benjamin Barnard, Jr., 1834, 1835, 1839.
Mark Batchelder, 1836, 1852, 1853.
Israel Batchelder, 1837, 1838.
John Davidson, 1840, 1841.
Freeman Lyon, 1842, 1843.
George Batchelder, 1844, 1845.
Jesse Rider, 1846.
Ezra Dodge, 1847, 1848.
Ira K. Batchelder, 1849.
Edward Batchelder, 1850, 1851.
F. P. Batchelder, 1854, 1855.
A. T. Byard, 1856, 1857.
Dexter Batchelder, 1858, 1859.
Joel Adams, 1860, 1861.
Edmund Batchelder, 1862, 1865.
Amos G. Bowker, 1863, 1864.
O. P. Simonds, 1866, 1867.
J. P. Long, 1868, 1869.
Jonathan Hapgood, 1870, 1871.
Hiram Griswold, 1872.
Charles Batchelder, 1874.
Wm. B. Simonds, 1876.
George K. Davis, 1878.
M. J. Hapgood, 1880.
John G. Walker, 1882, 1884.
James C. Lakin, 1886.
M. B. Lyon, 1888.

DELEGATES TO CONSTITUTIONAL CONVENTIONS.

Peter Dudley, 1814, 1821.
Josiah Barnard, 1828.
Samuel Stone, 1836.
Mark Batchelder, 1843.
Gen. S. Dudley, 1850.

MEMBER OF THE SENATE.

Ira K. Batchelder, 1850, 1851.

SIDE JUDGES.

Ira K. Batchelder, 1864, 1865.
Dexter Batchelder, 1888.

MAIL.

The first mail was carried from Chester to Peru on horseback by Francis Fuller of Chester as early as 1815 (or earlier), and for four years Peru was the end of the route, the carrier returning to Chester the same day. He passed through Andover, Weston, and Landgrove Flats, distributing newspapers from house to house. In 1819 the route was continued to Manchester, but it is not known how often it was carried, or by what route. In 1822 Simeon Leland established a line of daily stages from Charlestown No. 4 to Manchester, and Peru had a daily mail each way until 1851. At the introduction of railroads into Vermont the coach and four was discontinued, and a mail stage was run from 'Derry to Manchester one day, returning the next, and is in use at the present time. The postmasters were as follows: Reuben Bigelow, 1st.; Daniel Tuthill, 2nd.; Russell Tuthill, 3rd.; M. Smalley, 4th.; O. P. Simonds, 5th, 1839 to 1850; Cyrus Hatch, 6th, 1850 to 1851; O. P. Simonds, 7th, 1851 to 1866; L. B. Hapgood, 8th.; T. K. Snow, 9th.; C. W. Whitney, 10th.; G. K. Davis, 11th.; O. P. Simonds, 12th.; G. L. Richardson, 13th.

MILITARY COMPANIES.

A military company was organized in the town in 1805, with Peter Dudley, first captain, John Batchelder, first lieutenant, and the usual number of non-commissioned officers. The annual training was held on the first Tuesday in June. The captain issued his orders to the orderly sergeant, who delivered them to the corporals to warn the men on their lists to be on hand at the appointed time and save themselves from being fined. The commissioned officers were equipped with a military coat, with round brass buttons as large as a cherry, sash, epaulettes, sword, and a cockade hat with a tall plume in the top. The privates were equipped with a gun, bayonet, knapsack, canteen, cartridge box covered with leather, two spare flints, priming wire and brush. They usually had a fall training. A regimental muster, held within the bounds of the regiment, was held at Weston Island or 'Derry. In 1825 Brigadier-General Dudley had a brigade muster at Manchester. Joel Adams was baggage master for the company at Peru. The only rations furnished was a few gallons of New England rum, which was paid for by the commissioned officers in honor of their office, and the only pay that the soldiers received was their exemption from poll tax. All able

MARK BATCHELDER

bodied citizens over the age of 18 and under 45 were subject to
duty. One practice prevailed which would not be tolerated in these
days; the soldiers would be at the residence of the commissioned
officers any time after midnight on the morning of the training day
to wake up the officers, which was accomplished by the discharge of
their guns around the house, this being an invitation to the officers
to come out and treat, which was promptly done. These trainings
were kept up by practice and law until 1844, when the company was
disbanded. No one knows of any records of the company being in
existence. The captains were promoted to regimental officers or
discharged after three or four years service, which exonerated them
from military service, and the under officers were promoted by the
vote of the company. It was considered wrong to promote a lower
officer over a higher one, and it was not often done. The band
consisted of fifes, bass and tenor drums. The tenor drummers were
Mark Batchelder and Alfred Sawyer; bass drummer, Joel Adams;
fifers, Russell Wyman and Abel Adams. The captains of the
company were Peter Dudley, John Batchelder, James Lincoln,
Joseph Whitney, Israel Batchelder, Josiah Stone, Asa Simonds, Joel
Lyon, Mark Batchelder, Joel Adams, F. K. Stiles, Stephen Dudley,
and Ezra Dodge. The trainings were held on the common where
the old meeting house stood, and the soldiers were allowed to occupy
the church when necessary. The day was spent in calling the roll,
examining the equipments, drill, company marching, and closed with
a lively game of ball or a trial of the strong and active ones in
wrestling. The June training was about the best holiday that the
boys had during the year, and men of all ages would be present.
The boys, in imitation of their fathers, organized a company, elected
a full board of officers, who called out all the boys in town between
the ages of 14 and 18, and went through all the manoeuvres of the
older ones, handling the wooden guns with dexterity and a great
deal of ambitious pride.

NAMES OF SOLDIERS IN THE REVOLUTION WHO HAD A PENSION.

Peter A. Gould, Elijah Simonds, Benjamin Barnard, Sen.,
Stephen Bennett, David Sawyer, Ebenezer Stiles, Asa Farnum,
Moody Roby.

NAMES OF SOLDIERS FROM PERU WHO SERVED IN THE REBELLION.

Name.	Age.	Date of Enlistment.	Date of Muster.	Reg't.	Co.	Remark.
William S. Weymouth,	42	Oct. 16, '61,	Oct. 31, '61,	2	A	Died Dec. 14, '61.
Benjamin S. Barnard,	30	"	"	2	A	Discharged Nov. 7, '62.
Daniel M. Priest,	23	"	"	2	A	Discharged Oct. 31, '62.
Henry Stiles,	20	"	"	2	A	Promoted Sergeant Major, mustered out Oct. 31, '64.
Clark R. Bryant,	22	"	"	2	A	Mustered out Oct. 31, '64.
Harlan E. Batchelder,	22	"	"	2	A	Mustered out Oct. 31, '64.
Warren S. Bryant,	21	"	"	2	A	Mustered out Dec. 7, '64.
Charles M. Hapgood,	18	"	"	2	A	Mustered out Oct. 31, '64.
Everett E. Adams,	22	"	"	2	A	Deserted Aug. 17, '62.
Charles D. Robbins,	21	"	"	2	A	Discharged Feb. 14, '63.
Wilbur F. Bowker,	20	Dec. 17, '61,	Feb. 18, '62,	8	H	Killed at Port Hudson, May 27, '63.
Henry W. Crocker,	32	Dec. 27, '61,	Feb. 12, '62,	8	H	Killed at Port Hudson, June 15, '63.
Joseph M. Long,	18	Dec. 18, '61,	"	8	H	Discharged Nov. 20, '62.
Charles D. Odell,	23	Oct. 7, '61,	"	1	F	Discharged Aug. 2, '62.
Frank P. Simonds,	21	June 24, '62,	July 6, '62,	9	D	Discharged Aug. 29, '63.
Lysander W. Russell,	25	"	"	9	D	Discharged April 29, '63.
Schuyler Bennett,	24	Mar. 21, '62,	April 12, '62,	4	I	Mustered out July 13, '65.
John P. Quackenbush,	22	Dec. 8, '63,	Dec. 24, '63,	9	F	Died in service, April 29, '65.
Clarence B. Lincoln,	18	Dec. 9, '63,	Dec. 17, '63,	9	F	Died Oct. 3, '64.
Albert J. Simonds,	18	"	"	9	F	Mustered out in 1865, was kept for service some time.
Lauren A. Russell,	18	"	"	11	C	Died at Washington, Feb. 20, '64.

Name	Age	Enlisted	Mustered	Age	Co.	Remarks
Levi W. Collins,	18	Mar. 24, '64,	April 12, '64,	17	F	Mustered out July 14, '65.
John T. Howard,	18	Feb. 10, '64,	Feb. 10, '64,	17	F	Mustered out July 14, '65.
Thomas J. Lakin,	44	Dec. 9, '63,	Dec. 9, '63,	9	F	Discharged May 20, '65.
Phillip J. Johnson,	21	Jan. 26, '65,	Jan. 26, '65,	5	A	Mustered out June 29, '65.
Peter Willey,				4 Ms. U.S.N.		
James J. Howlin,						
Abel T. Wyman,	23	Mar. 31, '64,	Mar. 31, '64,	2	A	Sick in hospital, July 16, '65.
Calvin R. Bryant,	19	Aug. 4, '64,	Aug. 4, '64,	9	F	Mustered out June 13, '65.
Leroy G. Davis,	19	Sept. 5, '64,	"	2	A	Mustered out June 9, '65.
Richard Green,	30	Sept. 23, '64,	Sept. 23, '64,	9	F	Mustered out June 13, '65.
John W. Penfield,	19	Aug. 4, '64,	Aug. 4, '64,	9	F	"
William A. Penfield,	20	"	"	9	F	"
Obadiah N. Russell,	23	"	"	8	H	Mustered out June 1, '65.
Charles F. Sheldon,	24	Sept. 15, '64,	Sept. 15, '64,	5	F	Mustered out June 19, '65.
Gilman Thompson,	30	"	"	5	F	"
Joseph M. Farnum,	18	Sept. 20, '62,	Oct. 23, '62,	16	I	Mustered out Aug. 10, '65.
Jefferson French,	36	"	"			"
Jerome B. Lakin,	16	"	"			"
Joseph H. Mason,	42	"	"			"
Chas. H. Reed,	18	"	"			"
Wm. C. Strong,	46	"	"			"
George R. Wyman,	19	"	"			"

Joseph M. Farnum re-enlisted in the 5th Vermont, Company E., Sept. 1864, and was killed in the battle of Cedar Creek Oct. 19, 1864.

Hezekiah Stone and E. B. Batchelder furnished substitutes.

The nine months' volunteers received $100 as town bounty. They were at the battle of Gettysburg.

The first ten on the list of soldiers were enlisted by Col. J. H. Wallridge, and received no bounty, but the citizens gave each man ten or twelve dollars for spending money until they got into camp. They were accompanied to the depot on the morning of October 21, 1861, by friends who wished to give the shake of the hand and say the last good-bye as they parted, the friends for their vacant homes and the soldiers to the front to strengthen Company A of the 2nd Regiment. The captain of the company was William S. Weymouth, and he enlisted body and soul, but before they had reached their regiment his energy and spirits flagged, and he sank under the task that he had undertaken. In two months his remains were sent home and buried on December 16, 1861. Slowly and sadly was he carried to his grave to the music of the drums and fifes, accompanied by his family and a large number of friends and citizens. Benjamin S. Barnard and D. M. Priest were wounded before Richmond in the seven days battle of the Pines, taken prisoners and sent to Richmond. Barnard was put into Libby prison and kept there until he was so prostrated that he could not walk, when he was exchanged and sent to the Philadelphia hospital, staying there until he recovered. Priest was placed on an island by his own choice, where he could have the benefit of water but no shelter. He was discharged sooner than Barnard, but it was a sad experience for both of them. C. M. Hapgood was wounded by a bullet grazing his scalp, was sent home on furlough but soon returned to duty. The other five followed the army of the Potomac for three years and were in most of the battles, some of them not receiving a scratch or being away from duty a single day during that time.

Wilbur F. Bowker, Henry W. Crocker, and Joseph M. Long voluntarily enlisted December 21, 1861, and were mustered into Company H of the 8th Regiment. Bowker and Crocker went south with the regiment. Bowker was shot at Port Hudson May 27, 1863, and Crocker was shot June 15, 1863. They were both shot by sharpshooters, and were the first two that were killed in service from Peru. Joseph M. Long went into camp at Brattleboro, where he took cold and was sick. He had a furlough, but was discharged November 2, 1863, and afterwards died of consumption.

Allen J. Benson enlisted in Company C of the 11th Regiment, Heavy Artillery, and was taken prisoner. He died in Andersonville prison, Ga., August 21, 1864, and was the only soldier from Peru who died in prison.

Clarence B. Lincoln died in hospital of yellow fever October 3, 1864, in South Carolina.

Lauren P. Russell mustered into Company C of the 11th Regiment December 17, 1863, and died at Washington February 20, 1864.

Leroy Wyman enlisted December 19, 1863, was wounded, and died in hospital October 4, 1864.

John Platt Quackenbush enlisted December 8, 1863, and died in service April 29, 1865.

Of the forty-seven volunteers furnished by Peru, eight died in service.

SCHOOLS AND SCHOOLHOUSES.

The first school in town was taught by Reuben Bigelow in 1803, and was kept in Deacon Seth Lyon's log house, which stood in Mr. Whitney's lot. Schools have always been sustained since they were first started, but were held in private houses until 1807. James Grant taught several terms in the Holton house. The first school-house was built in 1807 in the corner of M. B. Lyon's lot, at the back of the barn south of the Adams road. It was a large building, with an L for the entrance, and was fitted up inside with two rows of wooden seats and a desk, with an open stove in the centre. This building was also used as a church, the desk answering the purpose of a pulpit, and the men sitting on one side of the room, while the other side was occupied by the women. Town meetings were held in the schoolhouse for a long time. James Grant, father of Gen. L. A. Grant, taught the first term of school in the building in 1808, and this was the only school that held winter terms until 1822. The building committee, Reuben Bigelow, Gen. Peter Dudley and Deacon Thomas Wyman, took great interest in having this house built, and they all had large families, which were sent there to be educated.

In 1810 a log house was erected about half way between Clark Lakin's house and the bridge to be used for a summer school. It was taught, at different times, by Hannah Barnard, Sally Ballard, Abigail Bigelow (she was 15 years of age when she taught her first term), Samantha Ballard, Lucinda Whitcomb, Lucinda Bigelow, and Lucy Dudley, who taught the last term held in the schoolhouse.

In 1821 the town was divided into three school districts, which were called the centre district, the north district, and the south district, and these were sufficient to accommodate all the scholars. The centre district retained the old schoolhouse until 1830, when a new one was built near where Freeman Lyon lives, which was kept until the present schoolhouse was built, the name of the district being then changed to district No. 3. The first winter school in the north district was held in a log house that had been built for a dwelling house, and was taught by John H. Dudley, who was an excellent teacher, for eight dollars a month. He also taught the second term, receiving ten dollars a month. The next year's school was held in a log house standing in the corner of Edgar Batchelder's lot, north of the road leading to Mr. Bell's place, and was taught by Russell Tuthill. In 1823 a frame house was erected on the site where the present house stands, and was enclosed on the outside with clapboards half an inch thick and six inches wide. There was a fireplace at one end of the room, benches made out of slabs, long tables made with plain boards, and one chair for the teacher. The boys and girls, who had just come from the log house, thought this a very convenient schoolhouse. Three years later this building was sealed up with spruce boards overhead, a closet and entry made, permanent desks and seats put in, and a teacher's desk was furnished. The scholars then thought that they had a grand schoolhouse, and many a pupil had the mind and intellect stored and polished so as to be intellectually brighter and stronger for life's work, and some were taught physically by the birch in a way that was not agreeable or pleasant for the time. Joseph Wright and Asa B. Brown were teachers in this school.

The south district had school kept in private houses owned by Elijah Simonds and Gen. Peter Dudley until 1822, when the district erected a house on the right hand side of the road east of Goodell Walker's house, in which many valuable terms were held. In 1833 this house was moved to the spot where the present schoolhouse stands, near Charles Russell's house. In 1838 the town was divided into six districts, and this changed the south district to district No. 1. The first schoolhouse that the district built was moved near Joel Adams's house, and school was kept in it until the present one was built in 1864. The old house is now standing at the west end of Mr. Adams's wood shed, and is used for a carriage house. It has seen much hard service, having been built about 80 years.

District No. 5 built their first schoolhouse in 1838, which was burnt down in 1864. The present building was erected in 1864, and is well built.

In 1838 district No. 6 built a schoolhouse, which is now in use. Previous to that they used Capt. Wait's house.

District No. 7, which is at the extreme north part of the town, was organized by I. K. Batchelder in 1866, and has a schoolhouse and school that does it great credit.

A school district was organized at the notch mill, and school kept in private houses. It has since been given up.

The first select school held in the town was in 1828, and was taught by Theodore Wilbur. It was exclusively a grammar school, and twenty-two students attended its session, very much to their improvement and satisfaction. Esquire Bigelow was the principal one in the organization of this school. In 1849 John P. Reynolds taught a select school with great success, and from 1850 to 1859 select schools were taught by Milton R. Tyler, George Richardson, S. E. Burnham, and Stephen Grout, which were a credit to the teachers and to the town. Since that time there have been several select schools, the most thorough of which was taught by Miss Nancy Haynes.

Peru has given commendable attention to her schools, and many good teachers have been brought up in town. Among the early teachers were the daughters of Reuben Bigelow, Gen. Dudley, Samuel Stone, J. Howard, Asa Simonds, B. Barnard, and among the young men were Joseph Wright, A. B. Brown, Wm. B. Lincoln, Hiram Howard, B. S. Ballard, I. K. Batchelder, Reuben Stone, who all taught school more than fifty years ago.

SCHOOL TEACHERS OF PERU.

Abigail Bigelow, Samantha Ballard, Sally Ballard, Lucinda Bigelow. Damietta Bigelow, Laura Bigelow, Orrella Bigelow, Caroline Bigelow, Betsey Warren, Asa B. Brown, Hepsibah Barnard, Nancy Barnard, Emily Barnard, B. L. Barnard, Seth B. Barnard, Emily Messenger, Joseph H. Simonds, D. K. Simonds, Peter Dudley, Lucy Dudley, Elvira Dudley, Joseph Wright, Lydia Dudley, Lucinda Whitney, James M. Dudley, B. S. Ballard, Sophia Simonds, Mary Simonds, Mary Wyman, Nancy Wyman, Louisa Holton, Harriet Howard, Olive Howard, Hiram Howard, Abigail Barnard, Lucy Barnard, B. L. Barnard, Marcellus Lyon, M. B. Lyon, Ruth Hapgood, Susan A. Burton, Mary Burton, Bowman Burton, R. Bigelow Burton, Ann Whitney, Susan Batchelder, John W. Batchelder, Wm. B. Lincoln, David Smith, Rosetta Stiles, Sarah Stiles,

Henry Stiles, Martha Stone, Susan Stone, Reuben Stone, Abbie Davis, Abbie Ann Davis, Ira K. Batchelder, F. P. Batchelder, Roxana Batchelder, Amos Batchelder, Daniel Davidson, Julian E. Batchelder, Rossetta Batchelder, Mary Emma Batchelder, Nellie Walker, Ellen Simonds, Jennie Byard, Blanche Simonds, Frank Wyman, Mary McMullen, Myron Dudley, George Dudley, Lucy Dudley, Ella Batchelder, Sarah A. Simonds, Mary Chandler, G. N. Wyman, A. P. D. Simonds, Ellen Simonds, Martha Simonds, Charlotte H. Hapgood, Marshall J. Hapgood, Carrie Adams, Rowena Baldwin, Isa Weymouth, Abbie Dale, Ann Janette Dale, Bell Simonds, Emily M. Mellendy, Aurilla Mellendy, Ella Mellendy, Eunice Chapin, Hannah Batchelder, Daniel Batchelder, Mary Coolidge, Chalmers H. Coolidge, James K. Batchelder, Luella Batchelder, Damietta Dudley, Caroline Dudley, Burton Barnard, Hannah Thomas, Abbie Davis, Ellen Davis, Helen Rider, Caroline Rider, D. M. Priest, Sarah Coolidge, Charles K. Batchelder.

COLLEGE GRADUATES WHO WERE NATIVES OF PERU.

R. B. Burton, Myron S. Dudley, D. K. Simonds, James K. Batchelder, Daniel M. Priest, Alonza Barnard, M. J Hapgood, Robert A. Ray.

ATTORNEYS WHO WERE NATIVES OF PERU.

Thomas Hill, practiced in Bangor, Me.

Moses Hill, practiced in Ohio.

Ezekiel Simonds, practiced in New Orleans, La.

James M. Dudley, practiced in Johnstown, N. Y.

D. K. Simonds, admitted to the bar.

James K. Batchelder, practiced in Arlington, Vt.

A. Clark Batchelder, practiced in Ayer Junction, Mass.

Charles W. Ray, practiced in Concord, N. H.

PHYSICIANS WHO WERE NATIVES OF PERU.

Horace Ballard, practiced in Williamstown, Mass.

T. Miles Bigelow, practiced in the West.

Asa B. Brown, practiced in Ohio.

Wm. B Lincoln, practiced in Ionia, Mich.

Hiram Howard, practiced in Ohio.

R. B. Burton, practiced in New York.

Asa Bigelow, practiced in Toledo, Ohio.

Daniel M. Priest, practiced in New York.

Charles W. Ray, practiced in Jamaica, Vt.

Joseph Wright, Universalist.
Moses Adams, Methodist.
M. S. Dudley, Congregationalist.
Alonzo Barnard, Congregationalist, missionary among the Indians.
Frank Goodrich, Methodist.
C. H. Coolidge, Congregationalist.
D. K. Simonds, editor of the Manchester Journal.

CHURCHES.

CONGREGATIONAL CHURCH.

The Congregational church was organized in 1807, when Benjamin Barnard and Lucy his wife, Thomas Wyman and Sarah his wife, Seth Lyon and Sophia his wife, and William Green and Betsey his wife were formed into church fellowship, and subscribed to the articles of faith. Rev. Mr. Fairley, pastor of the Congregational church in Manchester, and his delegate, Capt. Burton, were present on this occasion. Thomas Wyman was elected moderator and clerk of the church at this meeting.

March 20, 1808, Elisha Whitney, Dr. Silas Clark and his wife, Elijah Simonds and his wife, and Mrs. Lucy Hill were united to this church. The Lord's supper was administered by Rev. Mr. Fairley, of Manchester. Thomas Wyman and Seth Lyon were elected deacons.

On July 17, 1808, Rev. Mr. Calton, of Sandgate, administered the Lord's supper.

In 1809 it was voted to adopt the articles and join in fellowship with the western consociation, and Deacon Thomas Wyman was voted delegate to represent the church in consociation. New members continued to join the church each year until 1814, when the society numbered thirty-four persons. The Lord's supper was administered by pastors from neighboring towns on each side of the mountain. Occasionally a missionary would come from Connecticut or Massachussets to preach and visit among the people, also to receive new members into the church and hold a communion service.

In 1813 the members of the church extended an invitation to Oliver Plympton to be ordained and settled over the church as a permanent pastor, which he accepted. A council was called to meet at Deacon Wyman's house on the 28th day of December, 1813, for the purpose of ordaining Oliver Plympton to the work of preaching the gospel in Peru. The council consisted of Rev. Elijah Norton, Deacon Beriah Wheeler, delegate, Rev. James Tufts, Arba Holbrook, delegate from Wardsboro, Rev. John Norton, Deacon James McCormick, delegate from Windham, Rev. Amos Pettingil, and Deacon Asa Loveland, delegate from Manchester. Rev. Mr. Norton was elected moderator, and Rev. Mr. Pettingil scribe. The candidate presented the credentials of his standing in the church and his license to preach, was examined as to his doctrinal belief, his acquaintance with theology, and his qualification to preach the gospel. It was unanimously voted to accept him, and he was ordained in the centre schoolhouse, that being the place where the meetings were held. Rev. Mr. Lawton offered the introductory prayer and gave the right hand of fellowship; Rev. Mr. Tuft preached the sermon; Rev. Mr. Pettingil offered the ordaining prayer; Rev. Mr. Norton gave the charge and made the last prayer. This was a happy day for the society, and though there was no church, they had a schoolhouse which was well fitted for their use. Here they could meet for service with their first chosen and beloved pastor, with favorable prospects of enjoying the same for some time. But they were soon disappointed. Their pastor went to Wardsboro to get married (the bride's name was Sally Cook), but died the same day that the marriage was to have taken place. He was buried at Wardsboro, and many of his congregation went there to attend the funeral. Mr. Plympton, as first settled minister in town, was entitled to three lots of land which had been reserved for that purpose in the charter of the town, but previous to his death he had deeded this right to the Congregational society. Deacon Lyon was moderator and clerk of the church at this time.

The society continued to hold services without the aid of a pastor, the deacons taking the lead. Esquire Bigelow would read the sermons, and he led the singing for more than twenty-five years. A year never passed without observing a communion season or having some baptism services. Rev. Amos Bingham preached for the society for a little while in 1817, which was accepted by the congregation with great pleasure. Twenty-six new members were added to the church as the results of his labors. The congregation extended a call to him to settle with them as a permanent pastor, but it does not appear that he accepted the call. Mr. Bingham did much for the spiritual growth of the church, and his preaching, his life, and his instructions were referred to as long as his hearers and converts lived. The fruits of his labors still exist, though he and his hearers have passed away.

The following ministers and pastors have labored for and with the church since it was organized: Rev. Mr. Fairley, Manchester; Dr. Wm. Jackson, Dorset; Rev. Mr. Calton, Sandgate; Rev. Silas S. Bingham, missionary from Connecticut; Rev. Mr. Kellogg, missionary; Rev. N. Lawton, Windham; Rev. Mr. Davis, missionary, Berkshire; Rev. Mr. Parker, missionary; Rev. Mr. Preston, Rupert; Rev. Mr. Hitchcock; Rev. James Tufts, Wardsboro; Rev. Joseph Kitchell, missionary; Rev. Mr. Sargeant, Chester; Rev. Mr. Spaulding, Jamaica; Amos Bingham, Bennington; Rev. Mr. Haynes, Rutland; Rev. Mr. Parmerly, Granville; Rev. Mr. Coe, New Hampshire; Rev. Mr. Goodale, Grafton; Rev. Mr. White; Rev. Mr. Cheever, Mt. Vernon; Rev. Mr. Manning, Ludlow; Rev. Philetus Clark, Londonderry; Rev. Mr. Parsons, Manchester.

In July, 1825, Rev. Nathaniel Rawson commenced to labor with the church, and continued to do so until 1828, when for two years there is no record of any person preaching until 1830. There were only four new members added to the church from 1821 to 1829. These were years of anxiety to all true disciples of Christ, for the love of many waxed cold. Dissension existed, and much labor had to be performed in the way of discipline, which caused fresh trouble. The ordinance of the Lord's supper was administered each year excepting 1829, for which there is no record of any communion, baptism or preaching, but the deacons held services and continued the Sabbath school.

In the winter of 1830 Rev. Nathaniel Hurd, an evangelist from Tinmouth, came among the people, and a new energy was imparted to the members of the church. On the 3rd of May, at a regular church meeting, they voted to establish three weekly prayer meetings in different parts of the town, also to attend a monthly concert, and have in connection with it a monthly church meeting. At a communion season in 1830 seven persons, living in Dedham, Mass., were united to the church by letter, and they were a great help to the church, both by their means and active labor. In 1831 protracted meetings were being held in many towns, and several members of the church attended some of the meetings, bringing the spirit of revival away with them. In August, meetings were

appointed to continue five days, and many came from other towns to
help on the good work. Rev. Mr. Anderson, of Manchester, and
Rev. Mr. Kingsbury, of Jamaica, were present and preached, and
Rev. Cyrus Hudson, of Dorset, preached one sermon which took fast
hold of the people's minds. Rev. Stephen Martindale, of Wallingford, was present, and preached like a person filled with the Holy
Ghost. Men who had constantly kept away from the house of God
now came in, and young people came in from other towns, filling the
church to overflowing. It seemed like the house of God and the
gate of Heaven, and none left without feeling that they had
something to do to enter into the straight and narrow way, which is the
way to everlasting life. Mr. Martindale, in his last sermon, held up
the Bible, saying, this is my text, and he preached the truths of his
text in a way that would melt the hardest heart. It was like the
hammer on a flinty rock, or the two-edged sword. The fruits of this
meeting will last forever, and it would be impossible to measure the
results. Thirty-three new members joined the church during these
meetings. Mr. Hurd remained with this church three years, leaving
it strong in numbers and vigorous to work for the cause of God.

During the years 1833 and 1834 the people were supplied by
Rev. Bowman Brown and Rev. Justin Parsons. Mr. Brown labored
as a missionary with great success, holding many special meetings.
Rev. Mr. Tuttle, of New York State, came to assist him in these
meetings, and their united efforts were greatly blessed by the
addition of forty new members to the church. During these two
years the society, assisted by Rev. J. Parsons, purchased the
parsonage place, which consisted of twenty-five acres of land, a
small house and a barn. This property has been of much value to
the society, by helping them to sustain a pastor.

In the spring of 1835 Thomas Baldwin came to the society, and
received instructions for a short time from Rev. Justin Parsons
before entering into the work of the church. Mr. Baldwin had a
common school education, and worked on his farm and at his trade
until he was over thirty years of age, when he turned his attention to
the preaching of the gospel. He was a man of good common sense,
affable and sociable with all persons, and spiritually alive to the work
of the Master. He made a very acceptable pastor, and did much
to strengthen the cause of Christ in the town. After laboring as a
licentiate for a year, he was invited to settle as pastor over the
church, which he accepted. A council was called to ordain and

REV. A. F. CLARK

install him, consisting of Rev. U C. Burnap, of Chester, Rev. M. B. Bradford, of Grafton, Rev. Silas Hodges, of Ludlow, and Rev. Justin Parsons, of Weston, with their delegates. Mr. Baldwin was ordained June 15, 1886, Rev. U. C. Burnap preaching the sermon. Mr. Baldwin labored faithfully in season and out out season for ten years, and performed a great amount of pastoral labor among all the families in town; he was also instrumental in keeping up discipline in the church. He officiated at more weddings and funerals than any other man in town. Revival meetings were held in the autumn of 1842, when Rev. Mr. Warren, of Ludlow, came to assist Mr. Baldwin. Their united labors were greatly blessed by the great head of the church, and many were brought into the fold of Christ. During the ten years that Mr. Baldwin was pastor there were fifty-three new members added to the church. He left in the spring of 1845, to the regret of the society and the whole community, and with the satisfaction that he had done his duty to his Master well and faithfully.

Rev. A. S. Swift was pastor of the church for over two years, and during this time the new church was dedicated. Ten new members were added to the church in these two years.

In the spring of 1848 Rev. A. F. Clark came from New York State to be pastor of the church. He was a well educated man, in the full vigor of life, and having a wife that was well calculated to be a helpmate for a pastor, being Mary Simonds, of Peru. Mr. Clark entered upon the Master's work at once. He was elected moderator and clerk of the church, and performed these duties during the eleven years that he was pastor of the church. Mr. Clark preached the doctrines of the fathers a little more than some of the congregation cared to hear, but he raised his hearers to a higher level, elevating them in mind and thought. On receiving a call to be installed in the church, he accepted, and a council was called to meet for that purpose on the 10th of July, 1849. The council consisted of Rev. Cyrus Hudson, of Dorset, Rev. M. B. Bradford, of Grafton, Rev. J. Walker, of Weston, Rev. Thomas Baldwin, of Plymouth, and Rev. Reuben Hatch, of Windham, with their delegates. Rev. M. B. Bradford preached the sermon. There were forty-two new members joined the church during the time that Mr. Clark was pastor. He worked for the elevation of his people, both morally and intellectually, and took great interest in the education of all classes, giving private lessons in his own house.

He also aided in getting up and sustaining select schools, where those who could not go away to school might have better advantages than could be obtained at the common schools. There were better scholars in town during his time than were ever there before or since. He preached upon the necessity of keeping the Sabbath until his influence caused it to be generally observed by the whole community. Mr. Clark took great interest in the Sabbath school, ever seeking and encouraging the neglectful ones to come in. In the spring of 1859, in the midst of his usefulness, he resigned, and asked the society to unite with him in calling together a council to dissolve his pastoral relations with the church, which was very reluctantly done.

In November, 1848, Rev. R. D. Miller came as pastor of the church, and remained until September, 1864. Twenty-two new members joined the church during this time. He left of his own choice, but the people would have been pleased to have had him stay and continue his labors.

Rev. M. A. Gates, by the request of the people, came to Peru from Tinmouth in November, 1864, and entered at once upon his duties as pastor of the church. He labored successfully for the interests of the church and for the upbuilding of Christ's kingdom, and his labors were rewarded by new members joining the church from year to year. In January, 1868, a council was called to install him over the church, consisting of Rev. J. H. Thyng, of Derry, Rev. R. S. Cushman, of Manchester, and Rev. A. F. Clark, of Windham, with their delegates. The installation services took place on the 3rd of January, Rev. R. S. Cushman preaching the sermon. In 1867 the society voted that Rev. Mr. Tarleton should be sent for to help Mr. Gates in holding revival meetings, that spiritual blessings might be showered upon the members of the church. The labor put forth by all Christians was greatly blessed, sinners were convicted and converted, uniting themselves to the church of Christ. During the time that Mr. Gates was pastor of the church it admitted sixty-seven new members. In August, 1868, Mr. Gates sent in his resignation. A meeting was called for the purpose of considering his resignation, and it was voted not to accept it, but to join in calling a council to consider it. The council met on the 20th of August, when the following resolution was passed: Whereas, our pastor, Rev. M. A. Gates, has labored with us in the gospel ministry for the last four years, with the evident approbation of the great head of the church upon his labors, giving the word of life to the penitent, baptising our children, receiving the faithful into the church, and burying our dead as a devoted servant of Christ, and is now about to remove from us. Therefore resolved, That we cheerfully express to him our unwavering confidence in his moral and religious character, our affection for him as a faithful minister of our Lord Jesus Christ, and our desire that the blessing of God may attend him in all his future labors. The council voted to dissolve the relation of the pastor and church, cordially recommending Brother Gates to the confidence of the churches as a faithful and laborious pastor.

Rev. A. F. Clark, who was formerly pastor of the church, returned to perform the ministerial duties of the church on the 8th of November, 1868. He received eleven members into church fellowship. Mr. Clark closed his labors in the church in May, 1873, and went to Leverett, Mass.

Rev. S. H. Amsden came to take the pastorship of the church in June, 1873, and continued his duties until October 9, 1876. He admitted four new members during that time.

Rev. Charles Rockwell was pastor of the church from November, 1876, to May, 1878, and united six new members.

Rev. Charles Scott came to the church on June 9, 1878, and was pastor for nearly a year. He admitted four new members to the church.

S. L. Vincent came in November, 1879, as licentiate, and the society extended to him a call to settle with them as their pastor, which he accepted. A council was called to ordain and install him, consisting of Rev. A. C. Reed, of Manchester, P. J. Walker, delegate; Rev. J. L. Harrington, of East Dorset; J. L. Batchelder; Rev. P. S. Pratt, of Dorset, G. H. Williams, delegate; Rev. J. H. Flint, of Weston; Deacon Enoch Pease, delegate from North Derry; G. S. Hobart, delegate; Rev. V. M. Hardy, of West Randolph. The candidate was examined and installed, Rev. V. M. Hardy preaching the sermon. Rev. S. L. Vincent continued his labors as pastor of the church until October 15, 1882, when he asked to be dismissed. A mutual council of the society assented to it, and dissolved the connection between pastor and people. During his pastorate three were added to the church by confession and five were added by letter.

A Sunday school was organized in this society in 1818, and has been sustained ever since.

METHODIST.

The Methodist society was organized in Peru on the 22nd of February, 1822, and was called the Athens Circuit. The prominent members were Samuel and Josiah Stone, Francis Bennett, N. Whitney, with their families. Soon after they were organized they were changed from the Athens Circuit to the Weston Circuit. They held meetings in private houses, and their numbers slowly increased. About 1825 a quarterly meeting was held in the Congregational church, with a large number of the brethren from Landgrove and Weston, it being a large gathering for that time and place. They held services in the North schoolhouse, and frequently had preaching. In 1833 a committee was chosen to take into consideration the building of a church, and consisted of Samuel Stone, Francis Bennett, and F. K. Stiles. They went to work in earnest, and by June the frame was up, shingled, boarded, clapboarded, and windows in. It was used without any more being done to it until 1846, when a meeting was called to see about improving it, and a committee, consisting of John Whitney, Abel Adams, and James Lincoln, was chosen for that purpose. It was decided to move the church back from the road and put an addition on the east end for a porch and belfry. The slips were sold for enough to pay for the improvements, quite a number being taken by members of other societies. The church was finished in the fall, and has never been changed in any way since. George Batchelder made the improvements. Rev. C. R. Harding preached the dedication sermon. Meetings were held in this church with much enthusiasm, and prosperity attended the enterprise. It was changed about this time from Weston Circuit to the "Landgrove and Peru Charge." The minister in charge of the circuit would sometimes preach in this church, and at other times one of the circuit ministers would preach. This church and society has suffered in the same way as many of the churches in the rural towns of New England. It is depleted by death and removals until its active and prominent members have all passed away to sing the songs of Zion in the new Jerusalem, and none have come to fill their place in the house of God, in consequence of which, the church is suffering for want of repairs.

A Sunday school was established and maintained in this society for many years.

Some of the prominent families who helped to sustain this society and church were Samuel, Josiah, and Joseph Stone, F. K.

Stiles, Francis and Jonas Bennett, John, Zimri, and Z. Whitney, M. Roby, Nathan, Alvah, Ira, and William Whitney, James Lincoln, Elder Lilley, A. G. Bowker, Nahum, Benjamin, and Abel Adams, Samuel Stiles, Levi Batchelder, Harvey and Hezekiah Stone, James Lakin, and Adam Corbet.

CHURCH BUILDINGS.

The Congregational church and society, feeling the need of a suitable church building, commenced in earnest to obtain one. It seems that the whole town was united in the enterprise, almost every family putting a shoulder to the wheel by purchasing one or more pews, thus encouraging the work of building. In 1815 Gen. Peter Dudley and Capt. John Batchelder were chosen a committee to superintend the building of the church and carry the work along. They commenced on the work immediately, the people furnishing the timber and lumber as best they could. The master workman in framing was Capt. Whitman, of 'Derry. The men assembled to raise the frame, and one of the deacons was about to offer a petition for Divine blessings on the enterprise, when Rev. Pliny Fisk (afterwards a missionary to Jerusalem) unexpectedly arrived, and offered a most earnest prayer for the blessing of God to rest upon the enterprise and all the community after it was finished. The prayer was abundantly answered during the labors of Rev. Amos Bingham. The architecture of this church was of the plainest kind. It was a square building, about 40 by 50 feet, with a portico on the east end about 15 by 20 feet, and finished plain on the outside. The building had two rows of windows, and was clapboarded with the best of pine clapboards, which were painted dark yellow. There was a door at the east end of the porch, and a flight of stairs on the right as you passed in, which led into the upper story. On the south side, and near the main building, was another door and a flight of stairs leading to the upper story, also two doors in the centre to enter the main building, turning right and left to follow the aisle. The pulpit stood at the west end of the building, with a large window at the back of it, and was about ten feet high, spreading out at the top. The deacons seats were partly under the pulpit, and Thomas Wyman and Seth Lyon sat there for years. The pulpit was finished with paneled work, with trimming around it of the best lumber. A flight of winding stairs, with railings, on which the dominie could ascend to the rostrum, from whence he could see every one in the building. The pulpit was seven or eight feet long, rounded out in the centre so that the speaker could stand in it, with a raised place in front for him to rest his books when reading. The only furniture was a board seat. From this pulpit has been dispensed the words of Life to encourage the fainting ones to a higher spiritual life, and to be faithful in doing the Master's work, also to encourage those out of Christ to come to him by repentance and faith, to enter into his fold and live for and with him. In front of the pulpit was a round table, which was used for communion services. The gallery was on the sides of the room, with a row of pews on the outside, and long seats on the sides for the singers, who were directly in front of the pulpit, but could only be seen by a small portion of the congregation. There were sixteen wall pews and eight centre pews in the church. The wall pews were about eight inches higher than the centre ones. The pews were made about six or seven feet square, with doors, the seats being made with hinges. It was the custom to stand during prayers, turning the seats up to make more room, and at the close of the prayer there would be a good deal of noise, as the seats would come down with a bang. The work of finishing the inside was done by Capt. Webster, of Weston, and Joseph Dodge, of Peru, who were excellent workmen. The result was the best meeting house in town. The best pine was used in this work, and the rich color of the wood gave it a very good appearance, there being no paint used on the inside. Meetings were held in this building during the warm weather, the old schoolhouse being used in the winter as it could be heated better than the church. About 1831 a large stove was put into the church, making it comfortable for the winter months, but some of the people thought it so affected their heads that they could not sit in the building; they soon got over it however. The good mothers who had used their foot stoves from the beginning continued to use them, but instead of going to the nearest neighbor for coal they used those from the church stove. In 1830 Esquire Bigelow put a small stove in his slip. About this time a long row of horse sheds was erected, obeying the precept that the merciful man will be merciful to his beast. This continued to be the place of worship until 1846, and many a Christian has been spiritually fed from this desk, and many a person led to accept the offer of salvation through a crucified Saviour from the hearing of God's word unfolded in this house, and there are living in distant places many who turn their minds back to

this church in full remembrance of the scenes and seasons enjoyed
in their earlier days, and sigh when they know that they can never
enjoy them again. But the time had come when the place of
worship must be changed. Three-fourths of the congregation came
from the southern part of the settlement, and some of them came
quite a distance. A little village had sprung up near the centre of
the society, and as a matter of justice to the whole congregation the
church had to be moved. It was with much misgiving with some
that this temple was given up, but it could not be helped, and among
those most affected were the three Batchelder brothers, who had all
been liberal supporters by their means and time. To remove it one
mile further away from them was a persecution, as they thought, not
to be endured. After the frame of the new church had been put up
it was thought best to make use of the old one in building the new.
A committee of three disinterested parties from adjoining towns was
called to appraise the pews in the old church. J. J. Hapgood, the
contractor for the new church, said he would pay the appraised value
and take the old church. He took out the inside and used a good
deal of the lumber in the new building, the frame being sold to be
used in the town hall at Londonderry. The spot on which the old
church stood is hardly discernible now, but the common still
remains. In the winter of 1845 the society called a meeting and
agreed to build a new church in the village, choosing Mark
Batchelder, Joel Adams, Jr., and F. P. Batchelder building committee.
A plan was drawn for the church and a contract made with J. J.
Hapgood by the committee for him to build and finish it, according
to the plan, for one thousand dollars. This contract did not include
laying the foundation. The slips were priced for enough, or more
than enough, to build the church, and sold. The land was bought
from Charles Lyon, and work was commenced on the foundation the
4th day of July, 1845. Gen. Peter Dudley, who was one of the
building committee of the old church, was present to help lay the
corner stone, and took great interest in the work. The frame was
raised and the roof put on in July. A subscription was raised for a
bell, and what was wanting was paid by J. J. Hapgood. George
Batchelder was master mechanic, and with the aid of his brother
John, did all the work on the building, completing it in the spring
of 1846. It was dedicated in June, Rev. Dr. Wickham, of
Manchester, preaching the sermon. Rev. A. S. Swift was the pastor
of the church at this time. Dr. Wickham's sermon was very useful

in allaying the asperity of feeling in the minds of individuals who felt that the sacredness of the old temple had been invaded and removed. His text was, "The beauty of the present temple far exceeds that of the former." After speaking for some time on his text, he said to those who felt their rights had been intruded upon, "Brethren, you can and must transfer your minds and love from yonder church on the hill to this new tabernacle, where you may sit united brethren to enjoy the blessing of the gospel of peace, and commune with the Saviour in the gospel of peace as united brethren." The effect of this sermon was like pouring oil on troubled waters; the irritation of feeling subsided and grace prevailed, while union in action and feeling continued as a blessing to the church. Religious services have been held in this church ever since it was built. In the absence of the regular preacher the services would be conducted by the deacons. In 1835 the society purchased, with the help of Rev. Justin Parsons, a parsonage, with twenty-five acres of land. They built a house on the land, moving the old house for an L to the new one, and it was occupied as a parsonage until 1850, when Rev. A. F. Clark thought the house too small and too far away from the church. The society then bought the place where the present house stands, and drew a plan for the house, which J. J. Hapgood built for $400 and the old parsonage, including three-quarters of an acre of land. In 1853 a cyclone passed over this place which moved the west end of the church from the foundation, injuring it more or less; it also carried the parsonage eight feet southerly and several feet easterly, leaving it balancing over the cellar. The family was in the house at the time, but no one was hurt. The frame being very strong it did not fall, but a good deal of the plastering cracked and fell. Mr. Lawrence, of Weston, was employed to put the house on its foundation, and, with the help of some of the citizens, had it finished in two days. The meeting house sheds and the parsonage barns were blown down, and part of the hotel roof was blown off. This gale came up in a black cloud, passed over quick and was gone. It came from the north-west, went south-east over I. K. Batchelder's pasture, and tore up some trees in his wood lot, where its force seemed to be spent. A recess for the singers was put behind the pulpit in the west end of the church, which makes good seats for the singers but does not add to the beauty of the building.

MECHANICS.

Asa Bailey was the first carpenter in town, and lived on the place west of Jonathan Hapgood's farm. It is supposed that he built the first frame building in town. He was the master workman in erecting Gen. Dudley's house, which was the first two-story house in town, it being clapboarded with riven and shaved clapboards.

Joseph Dodge was a good workman as a joiner, and his best job was on finishing the meeting house. He lived on the place where Charles Batchelder now lives until 1818, when he left town.

Nathan Whitney came from Athol, Mass., in 1819, and was a carpenter. He built most of the houses that were put up in the town for some years, his son Alvah working with him. Nearly one half of the buildings in town in 1837 were put up by the Whitneys, but they left town about that time. W. W. Whitney and his son Charles have done considerable mechanical work in town.

Edward Messenger came from Dedham, Mass., in 1829, and worked at the carpentering and joining business until his death in 1881. He was a good mechanic, and could turn out as much work as any man in town.

George Batchelder, a native of Peru, served his apprenticeship in Massachusetts. He came back and worked at his trade for fifteen years. Mr. Batchelder was the best mechanic that ever lived in town.

John W. Batchelder learned his trade from his brother George, and was a good workman. He left town about the time that he became of age and lived several years in East Dorset, but afterwards entered the stone business at Detroit, Mich. He died in 1890.

James Wait and Eben Tuttle were both carpenters and joiners, and did considerable work outside of the town. Two of Mr. Wait's sons, Harrison and Nelson, are mechanics, Harrison working in East Dorset, and Nelson in Weston.

E. P. Chandler was a carpenter and joiner.

Isaac Hill was the first blacksmith in town, and his shop stood on the spot where M. B. Lyons's south barn stands.

Royal Bryant's father worked in the Bigelow shop that stood in the corner of the Adams road. Joseph Howard worked in the same shop.

Mark Batchelder was a blacksmith, and worked at the business for over thirty years.

Royal Bryant worked at the blacksmith's trade in different shops for a number of years.

Lyndon Jenkins used the shop near Haynes's mill for a blacksmith's shop.

Royal Bryant's four sons worked in their father's shop at different times. Mr. Walker is now working in this shop.

Jesse Warren and Hiram Messenger did some blacksmithing in connection with the furnace business from 1829 to 1833.

David Sawyer, Stephen Bennett, William Green, William B. Lincoln, Amherst Messenger, Cyrus Staples, F. P. Batchelder, and Charles Batchelder have all been in the shoemaking business.

Esquire Bigelow worked in his own shoe shop.

O. P. Simonds, a veteran shoemaker, worked at the trade for more than fifty years.

MILLS.

The first saw mill in town was built in 1803 by the efforts of fourteen men. It was erected on the Chandler brook, about 150 rods below the bridge. Three dams had to be built before they had one that would hold the water. The mill was called the Federal Mill, and did a good business. It was of great use to the inhabitants, making the lumber that grew in that vicinity more valuable. The mill and dam were washed away one night in 1816, but no one knew it was gone until one of the workmen, who had started to go to the mill as usual, reported that he could find no trace of it. It was a great loss and drawback to the inhabitants. After this the people in the south part of the town had to take their lumber to a mill in Winhall, and those in the north part to Utley's mill in Landgrove.

In 1820 the three Stone brothers built a mill on the site where the Haynes mill now stands. This mill was thoroughly built, and did a large business, very much to the advantage and prosperity of the town. In 1828 Samuel and Josiah Stone bought out Joseph's share. They then put in a grist mill, quarrying the mill stones from a ledge in Landgrove, and also put in turning works for making chair stock. They did a good business until 1836, when they sold out to Oliver Wyman, who kept it a year or two. In 1837 the mill was damaged by heavy rains, and Mr. Wyman sold out to Isaac G. Long, who repaired the mill and dam. Mr. Long and his sons carried on the business several years, and then sold it to Holland

Tarbell. He built a new mill and made another dam lower down
the brook, also building the house and barn east of the mill. Mr.
Tarbell died before these improvements were all completed, and the
place was bought by James L. Haynes, who came from Fitchburg,
Mass. He completed the mill, and did considerable business in
the sawing line. After a few years he enlarged it and put in
circular saws, also putting in machinery for turning chair stock. It
is now owned and carried on by C. W. Whitney & Son, and is
doing a large business.

Asa Simonds built a mill, about 1827, near Ira. R. Walker's
place. For a time this mill had a run of stone for grinding. It was
sold to B. S. Ballard in 1841, who put in a large breast wheel and
did a good business for several years. George Batchelder and
Edward Batchelder owned and carried on the mill for a time.
Gustave Albee owned it a short time, but sold it to Elijah Simonds.
Mr. Simonds repaired the wheel and put in new machinery. He
died and his heirs sold the place to J. G. Walker. The mill is still
standing, but it is in a very dilapidated condition.

In 1836 a mill was built by James Wait in the north-east part of
the town, which has done, and is still doing, a good business. This
mill is now owned by Jackson Chadwick.

Shepherd Aldrich owns and runs a mill, and is doing a good
business.

In 1842 E. H. Tuttle built a mill in District No. 6. It has
changed hands a good many times, but is now doing a good
business. There is an engine connected with this mill.

H. Gould erected a mill in 1840, and did some business. It
afterwards went into the hands of Sarel Sawyer, who built a new mill
and put in modern machinery. Different parties have since owned
this mill. It was burned down in 1887, but a new mill was erected,
which is doing a good business at the present time.

The notch mill, so called by its being situated in the notch of
the mountains at the junction of two creeks, these creeks forming
the Mad Tom, was built in 1849 by Ira Cochran. He pushed his
way up to this spot over almost unsurmountable obstacles. Ira
Cochran and M. Manley sawed out many thousand birch ties for
the railroads. They were two miles up the mountain with no road
on which to draw their lumber, but they conceived the idea of
making a spout and running the lumber down by water. A spout
was made with planks, well nailed together, and two miles long. By

these means they could get lumber to the railroads in four days, and
the spout soon paid for itself. It was used for years in taking
lumber to the depot. Cochran & Manley bought several hundred
acres of land with all the timber on it, and carried on the business
for two or three years, in which time they built several houses and
barns around the mill. About this time a road was made to the mill
and it looked as though there was going to be a big business done
on the mountain. Cochran & Manley sold the property to James B.
Wood, of Concord, Mass., who carried on the business for ten or
twelve years. After that time the mill was owned by several parties.
Maltbey & Co., of Connecticut, bought the mill, with all the land
that could be procured in the vicinity, built large oval shaped kilns
of brick, hooped with iron, and began making charcoal. The land
was soon cleared of its original growth of timber. Many tenement
houses had been built in the vicinity of the mill, and it was about
this time that School District No. 8 was organized. There is no
business done now in this part of the town, and the buildings are all
decaying, but a new growth of timber is springing up all over this
section.

Barnum & Co. bought a large tract of land on the mountain in
the south-west part of the town, near the turnpike, and manufactured
charcoal as long as the wood lasted. This charcoal was all sent to
Connecticut. There is yet a large quantity of timber in the northwest part of the town, but it is slowly diminishing.

About 1852 Daniel Davis commenced to build a mill on the
stream east of the Byard farm. He made a dam, erected a frame,
and built a small house. In the spring of 1853 Mr. Davis hung
himself in his own house, and the mill was then sold to Mark
Batchelder and C. F. Long. They finished building it and carried
on business there for some time. Coolidge & Spaulding began to
repair it some years later, but did not do any business there. It is
now in a very dilapidated condition.

About 1847 Dana Wyman built a mill on the brook that runs
through Albert Simonds's farm, west of John Walker's house. He
did business there several years. It was burnt down one night
without any one seeing the flames, and Mr. Wyman then built a new
mill. Charles Barnard and Burkitt Simonds owned and carried
on business in this mill for some time. Nahum Russell and Allen
Benson bought the place and improved it. It was last in the hands
of Almon Patterson. There is no business done in this mill at the
present time.

M. B. Hapgood erected a steam mill on the mountain, north of George Russell's place, which was burned down. A new mill was built and a good business done, the lumber being easily taken to the depot.

A steam mill was built on the mountain north from the Dickerson place, but was only run a short time.

An engine was put into the Sawyer mill, and a good business done there. This mill was burned down, but has since been replaced. At this time there were six steam mills doing business in Peru.

HOTELS.

The first hotel in town was built by Jonathan Butterfield on the summit of the mountain, and on the old road to Manchester. Mr. Butterfield carried on business in this house several years. It was run a year or two by Mr. Fairbanks, and several other parties carried on the business for short periods. In 1816 the turnpike road was completed and the old road abandoned, which made this hotel of no use.

Reuben Bigelow began to keep an hotel about 1807, and continued it until the new road was opened.

Esquire Tuthill and his son Russell built the brick tavern in 1822. They carried it on until 1835, doing a good business, and then sold it to L. McMullen, who kept it himself a year or two. He rented it to Mr. Smalley, F. Lyon, L. Howard, and Hiram Messenger, but finally sold it to Charles Lyon. R. Gibson next bought the place, and then sold it to Leonard Howard. Edward Batchelder owned this hotel and carried on business there for a time. In 1870 it was bought by G. K. Davis, who is the present owner. It is now known as the Bromley House, and is the only hotel between 'Derry and Manchester. A good business is done in this hotel, and it is the right place to find a good dinner.

Benjamin Barnard kept an inn from 1814 to 1839, when he took down his sign.

In 1831 Hiram Messenger opened a hotel on the height of land on the turnpike road, and carried on business there for ten or twelve years. Alexander Leland rented it for two years, and J. G. Mellendy owned and occupied this place. In 1856 Mr. Mellendy sold it to Mr. Dickinson, whose heirs now occupy it.

STORES.

In 1816 Warren Wyman kept a small assortment of goods in the old house on M. B. Lyon's place, but did not continue it long.

About 1827 J. J. Hapgood commenced business in the same building that the Hapgood store is now in. His business was small at first, his wife attending to it while he worked on the farm. His business increased from year to year, and he soon had a good sized country store, well filled with goods. The firm became J. J. & L. B. Hapgood, and it continued to do a prosperous business until 1870, when it was bought by T. K. Snow & Co., who kept it about a year. David Arnold leased this store for a short time. In 1874 J. J. Hapgood and M. J. Hapgood went into partnership and carried on business under the name of J. J. Hapgood & Co. They sold out to Richardson & Leonard in 1885.

In 1841 Francis Bennett put in a small stock of goods in the Bryant house, but sold out in 1843.

Charles W. Whitney & Co. carried on the store business for a short time, closing up about 1865.

William E. Polly erected a store opposite the hotel in 1856, and entered into the mercantile business. It proved unsuccessful, and the store was closed.

About 1872 J. P. and C. H. Long opened a store west of the Haynes' mill, and continued the business five years, when they sold the store and goods to M. J. Hapgood.

CASUALITIES.

Ezra Wyman, son of Deacon Thomas Wyman, was killed by the falling in of a clay bed as he was digging clay in the brickyard. This occured in 1816. He was 16 years of age.

Thomas H. Hall was killed by the falling of a tree in District No. 6, near James Wait's place, about 1836.

Mr. Thompson was killed about 1835 by a falling tree. He was at work on the Nourse farm.

Deacon Asa Simonds drove under a shed at the Manchester depot to escape a violent storm, and the shed fell on him. He was carried into the depot, but died two or three days after.

A. P. D. Simonds was killed by a mowing machine in 1867. He stepped between the horses that were attached to the machine, but lost control of them, they dragging the machine over him.

Harlan E. Batchelder went to his barn one night in 1868 to get his horse, and received a kick in the bowels. He died soon after from the effects of the blow.

Daniel Davis hung himself about 1852 in the house that stood near the mill.

BUILDINGS WHICH HAVE BEEN LOST BY FIRE.

Joseph Barnard's house, which stood on the spot where G. K. Davis's garden now is, was burned about 1823. Mr. Barnard's mother was the only person in the house at the time, and it was with difficulty that she escaped. No insurance.

In 1824 the dwelling house of Deacon David Simonds was burnt. There was no insurance but the good will of friends and citizens, who turned in to assist in building a new house and furnishing what was needful.

Scammel Burt's dwelling house, which stood east of David Simond's house, was burnt about 1825. He then built a house near Stowell Barnard's place, receiving assistance from the whole community.

Edmund Batchelder's barn, which was full of hay and grain, was struck by lightning and burnt in 1843. Insurance $100.

Joseph Stone's barn was struck by lightning and burnt in 1845.

Mr. Lathrop's dwelling house, which was on the Hull farm, was burned down about 1854.

The schoolhouse in District No. 5 was burnt in 1864, with all the school books.

John Howard's dwelling house on the Notch road was burnt.

All the large buildings on the Dudley farm, belonging to S. L. Walker, were struck by lightning and burnt in 1882. This was the most destructive fire the town ever had.

Dana Wyman's mill, which stood east of Burkitt Simond's place, was burnt.

All the buildings on the French farm were burnt in 1879.

J. Q. Adams's house was burnt in 1881. This house was in the village.

M. J. Hapgood's steam mill on the mountain was burnt in 1885.

Jacquith & Bryant's steam mill was burnt in 1887.

Nelson Weatherbee's buildings, which stood on the Staples place, were burnt in 1884.

J. L. Haynes's mill, with all the tools and machinery, was burnt in 1888.

M. J. Hapgood had two barns and sheds burnt in 1888. It is supposed that some one did it intentionally.

EPIDEMICS.

This town, situated as it is on the east and south slope of the mountain, ought to be, and is, a healthy location. Epidemics prevailed during the years of 1812 and 1814, many of the families suffering to an alarming degree, and almost every house was a house of mourning. The disease was called by some spotted fever, and by others typhus fever. To show the fatality of the disease, we give one case, which is furnished by Mrs Abigail (Bigelow) Whiting, who is now living in Chester, Vt.: "In the family of Philemon Parker four died with this fever. They occupied a log house of one room. I was fifteen years old at this time, and with another person, watched by the bedsides of the sick ones. The four were perfectly unconscious, and did not live long, dying in the order in which they were born, as follows, Jonas, aged 24 years; Nathan, aged 22 years; Susan, aged 20 years, and Anna, aged 18 years. Mrs. Parker had the disease about this time, and never fully recovered. She died a few months after of consumption. The family was attended by Dr. Chandler, who bled his patients copiously at that time."

In 1814 the fever again prevailed, and many suffered. Esquire Bigelow, his wife, and six children were stricken down, but only one of them died, a girl six years old. Dr. Gray attended this family. There has been no prevailing sickness in town since this, and generally speaking, it is an healthy town.

In 1825 Samuel Stone and his seven children had the typhus fever. They all recovered but one son, who was 17 years of age. The mother of this family did not have the fever.

In 1850 the typhus fever prevailed in the family of John H. Sawyer. He and his nine children were sick with it at the same time. Mr. Sawyer and two of his sons died. No other family in town had the disease at this time.

About 1856 the family of Stephen Tuttle were sick with typhus fever, Mr. Tuttle and two or three of the children dying. A little girl who had lived with this family six months before the fever broke out, died about this time, but no other member of the family where she was living at the time had it.

In 1844 the smallpox broke out in the family of Whittimore Thomas. Mr. Thomas lived in a house on the opposite side of the road from Freeman Lyon's house, near the east schoolhouse. Seven of the children were taken singularly sick, and Mr. Thomas called in a Thompsonian doctor to attend them. On the third visit the doctor said he should think the disease was smallpox, and wanted to know where they had been exposed to it. Mr. Thomas, who had recently come from the West, told the doctor that he felt a little unwell at the time he reached home, and on examination it was found that he had brought the disease with him. The selectmen called Dr. Chandler, of Andover, who was skilled in diseases, and he agreed with the first doctor. Two other families were taken down by visiting the sick ones. Twelve persons had it in the town, but all recovered. Palmer Rollins, a young man, imprudently exposed himself to it and went to Keene, N. H., where he died.

DOCTORS.

The first doctor who lived in town was Dr. Silas Clark, who came from Winhall in 1808, and settled in the south part of the town. His log house was on the farm now owned by C. H. Russell, on the old road north of Russell's house. He did not have a very large practice, as the population was not numerous at that time. He was an active Christian, and helped a great deal to make the town prosperous. His wife died of the epidemic in 1814, and he then went to Herkimer County, N. Y., where he married his second wife.

Dr. C. P. Hatch came into town in 1847, from Alstead, N. H. He was a well educated man, and very successful in his business. Mr. Hatch married Mrs. S. A. (Burton) Chamberlin, of Peru. After a short time he moved to Acworth, N. H., much to the regret of his many friends.

Dr. D. H. Marden succeeded Dr. Hatch, coming into town in 1850. He was a man of active habits, and did all the business that there was to be had. Dr. Marden was a very successful farmer, and filled up his spare time at that business until he left town. He moved to 'Derry in 1868, where he now resides. Mrs. Marden and four of the children died of consumption in 'Derry.

Dr. Charles Chandler, of Andover, and Dr. Henry Gray, of Weston, were called to practice in town, and did a large share of the business until 1830. Their professional skill was acquired more by practice than by study.

Dr. Amori Benson settled in Landgrove about 1825, and practiced medicine in that town and Peru for forty years, doing a good business.

Dr. L. G. Whiting, of Derry did a successful business in town until he moved to Chester. Since that time he has often been called to consult with the town doctors on important cases.

Dr. Barker succeeded Dr. Whiting at Derry, and did a good business in Peru until his death.

There is no physician in town at the present time, and when needed are called from Derry or Manchester.

CEMETERIES.

There were several grown persons and children buried in the south-west corner of the Holton lot. A few of the oldest residents can remember mounds, with plain headstones, in this place, but it has now been all ploughed over.

The north cemetery was given to the town by Richard Stratton in 1803. It was first enclosed by a board fence, the present wall being built by voluntary workmen.

The south cemetery was bought of Joel Adams for one hundred dollars. Asa Phillips was the first person interred in this cemetery, in 1857.

BIOGRAPHIES.

Reuben Bigelow, a native of Westminster, Mass., came to Bromley in 1797, and commenced new on the land known as the Bigelow farm. He built his first house and barn on the hill south-west from the present buildings. Mr. Bigelow married Abigail Brooks, of Princeton. On the first of March, 1800, he moved his wife and two children into Bromley. In 1806 the road was altered, and he moved his buildings to a more favorable position, when he opened a tavern. He was a strong man, both physically and intellectually, and one who was well calculated to build up society and lead in all departments of life. Mr. Bigelow was proprietors' clerk, taking part in the division of land into lots. At the organization of the town he was appointed as one of the officers, and held some office every year until his death. He was town clerk and treasurer from 1812 to 1834, was also one of the first justices elected, which office he held all through his life. He had the honor of being the first representative of the town to the general assembly, filling this office several terms, also of being the first postmaster. Mr. Bigelow always took an active part in building up and sustaining the society and church, though not a member, and read the sermons when the meetings were conducted by the deacons. He was active in sustaining schools, and well he might be, having three sons and nine daughters to educate. Most of his children were educated for teachers, and the oldest daughter taught school from the time she was 14 years of age until she was 35, teaching thirteen years in Virginia. Two of the sons were educated for physicians, one of them, Dr. Miles Bigelow, died young in the Far West, and the other, Dr. Asa Bigelow, died at Toledo in 1888, aged about 67 years. The other members of the family, with the exception of one who died in Manchester, Vt., went west and south. A reunion of the eight living members of the family was held at the home of Mr. and Mrs. Willard (Mrs. Willard was a daughter of Demietta Tuthill) in Anna, Ill. This was the first time that the survivors of the family had been together for fifty years. Their names were Abigail, Lucinda, Deborah, Demietta, Laura, Orrilla, Caroline, and Asa, whose united ages were 520 years, averaging 65 years each. In May, 1887, the combined ages of the living members of this family was 632 years, averaging 79 years each. Abigail (Mrs. Whiting) died in 1887, aged 92 years, and Dr. Asa died in 1887, aged 67 years, six of the family being still alive. The longevity of this family exceeds that of any other in town.

Esquire Bigelow commenced to keep a hotel about 1810, and continued it until the travel was diverted away from his house by new roads. He introduced the business of making chairs, and never left it until he died. The chair shop was erected on the brook on the east part of M. B. Lyon's land, and he also had shops near his house. Mr. Bigelow employed workmen to do the manufacturing, doing the painting and varnishing himself. He sent his goods to Troy, N. Y., where they were sold. He had a shoemaker's shop and a blacksmith's shop, where he kept men busy all the time. At his death the business was brought to a close, and there is nothing left to mark the spot where his shops and store houses stood. Mr. Bigelow was a great advocate of temperance, and although he sold liquor at the time that he kept the hotel, he would not have it in his own house. Though always a conservative man in his business affairs, he was still a man of progression and improvement. Mr. Bigelow's personal appearance was noble and commanding, and would insure the attention of all persons that he came in contact with. His well chosen words made him an agreeable and pleasant companion in all his social intercourse with his associates.

General Peter Dudley was a man strong of body and mind. His early education was limited, but what he lacked in education he made up by his strong will and native energy. He was a man of the Ethan Allen stamp, with an inspiring way of overcoming, with resolute determination, all obstacles, and conquering all difficulties. Gen. Dudley did a good deal towards building up society in the town. He was born in Littleton, Mass., in 1773, and came to Peru in 1801, when he commenced the laborious work of clearing the land of timber and preparing it for cultivation. A log house was next built, and his wife came to share with him the hardships of the early settlers. In due time the log cabin was replaced by a large two-story house, which was clapboarded with split and shaved clapboards. This was the first two-story house in town, and was the homestead of the Dudley family for more than half a century. Mrs. Dudley, whose maiden name was Lucy Barnard, was a devoted, helpful and pious wife, highly respected by all who knew her, and greatly beloved by her family. She died on August 24, 1840, and her husband followed her on August 18, 1847. Gen. Dudley was in many respects a remarkable man. His integrity and force of character was well illustrated in the building of the Peru turnpike. A company was incorporated to build the Peru turnpike from Peru to Manchester. The contract was given to Mr. Atkins, Gen. Dudley being bondsman for him to the company that the work should be done in the specified manner and time. Atkins commenced the work, but kept drawing money from the company until he had received almost the whole of the contract price. He then took his departure, leaving Gen. Dudley to settle with the company. The company exacted the penalty of the bond, and without hesitation or evasion, Gen. Dudley went to work and finished the road at his own expense. This, however, made quite an inroad in his property. He was employed by the company to keep the road in repair for more than twenty years, and by his industry and economy he made

GEN. STEPHEN DUDLEY

up what he had lost, accumulating a comfortable property for himself and family. Gen. Dudley was liberal in his religious belief, yet did considerable towards the support of society, and was one of two committees for building the first church in town. He was one of the first justices, which office he held for a long time, and was also elected representative for nine terms. His military career was his glory, and he spent time and money freely for building up military affairs in Vermont. His first commission was that of captain in his own town, and he was promoted from one office to another until he became Brigadier-General, closing his military career with a brigade muster at Manchester about 1825.

Deacon Thomas Wyman came from Princeton, Mass., to Peru, in March, 1801, with a family of five children. He lived on his farm until his wife died, when he moved to Landgrove and lived with his son. Deacon Wyman was an active, useful man, of a sanguine temperament, and whatever he entered into to do was done at once. He did much to build up the institutions of the town, and was elected to all the important offices. Mr. Wyman was chosen deacon of the church at the time it was organized, holding the office for nearly thirty years, and, in the absence of a minister, leading the meetings. One morning in December, in 1844, he went into the woods to work, and on not returning at night the family became alarmed and went in search of him. They found him lying beside a log, dead, but without any external injuries. He was 82 years of age at the time of his death.

Thomas Wyman, Jr., son of Deacon Wyman, was the first child born in town. He received his education at the common school, and entered upon an active life of business. Before he was thirty years of age he was attacked with a difficulty from which he never fully recovered, but by prudence and care he was able to do light work. Mr. Wyman married Louisa Persons, of Weston, who died some years before he did. He was a useful member of society and a good citizen. He died at the age of 78 years.

Deacon Seth Lyon came to town from Princeton, Mass., in 1803, with a family of six children, and cleared a new piece of land. He was a strong man, both physically and intellectually, and well fitted to enter upon life in a new country. He was a good type of the New England yankee, laboring for the improvement of the town and the elevation of its inhabitants, filling many offices of trust. Mr. Lyon was elected deacon of the church with Deacon Wyman, and long assisted in leading the services in the sanctuary. He had a kind of a stereotyped prayer which he used to offer in his public services, and which has been remembered by many from childhood to old age. One sentence was, "We hew out to ourselves cisterns, broken cisterns which can hold no water." Deacon Lyon was a man well read in the scriptures. He died at Peru in 1844, aged 82 years. Mrs. Lyon then went to reside with her son Joel, where she died at a very old age.

Freeman Lyon was the oldest son of Deacon Seth Lyon, and came to Peru in his boyhood with his parents, receiving his education at the first school kept in town. He was a man of giant strength, and would cut a large log quicker and smoother than any other man in town. Mr. Lyon was chosen justice of the peace, constable, selectman, and twice elected representative to the general assembly. He died in Landgrove and was buried in the north cemetery in Peru, where his son Charles has erected a fine monument to his memory.

Joel Lyon came to town in his young days with his father, Deacon Seth Lyon, and received his education at the common school. He was a useful citizen, and held many town offices. Mr. Lyon was very conservative in his way of thinking, and filled the offices that he was intrusted to with prudence and care. He married Jane Batchelder, of Peru. In 1878 they celebrated their golden wedding, and large numbers of friends and relatives were present to congratulate them, leaving many tokens of respect. Soon after this Mr. Lyon received a fall which caused his death. He died in 1878, aged about 80 years, and his widow died in October, 1889, aged 85 years. Mrs. Lyon was the oldest child of her grandfather's family of ten children.

Mark Batchelder, oldest son of Capt. John Batchelder, was born in Mt. Vernon, N. H., in 1803, and came to Peru with his parents when a child. He received a common school education, and worked on his father's farm until he became of age, when he went to Grafton, Vt., to learn the blacksmith's trade. After he had served his apprenticeship he came back and commenced business in a shop which he had built near the residence of O. P. Simonds. A year or two later he moved to Charlestown, N. H., where he worked at his trade until 1831. He then came to Peru and bought the place from Deacon B. Ballard, and lived on it until 1836, when he bought the Oliver Wyman farm, where Albert Simonds now resides. In 1841 he had a new house built in the village, in which place he lived until

MRS. BENJAMIN BARNARD.

BENJAMIN BARNARD

he died. Mr. Batchelder was a good mechanic, and worked at his trade about 25 years. He was a good neighbor and citizen, and was always ready to attend to the wants of the community, both in sickness and death. He held several town offices, was elected delegate to the constitutional convention, and member of the legislature at different times. Mr. Batchelder married Rooxbury Conant, of Grafton, who died at Manchester at the age of 90 years. He died in June, 1863, aged 60 years.

Benjamin Barnard, Jr., came into town with his parents from Westminster, Mass., in 1800. At twenty-one years of age he commenced working for different persons by the month or day. In 1804 he married Rachel Philbrick, and lived in a log house which he built on the farm where Josiah H. Whitney lives. His wife died when they had been married about a year, and he then married her sister, Hepsibath Philbrick. He cleared his land, and soon had a farm which produced good crops. In 1812 he built a frame house where the present house stands, and put up a barn. Soon after this the turnpike road was completed, and he then opened his house to the public as an inn. Although the house was not very large, it was well patronized, and brought in a revenue without a great outlay of time or money. Mr. Barnard's motto was, "Time is money," and as he lived up to it he soon had a surplus which he could loan to his townsmen, much to their gratification, and his gain. He was strictly honest, giving every man his due and claiming the same himself. He kept his hotel until 1835. Mr. Barnard was a kind of a banker for that region when state banks were few and far apart. He took an interest in all the affairs of the town, and held several town offices, being elected selectman a good many times. At the last town meeting that he attended, which was in March, 1864, he said he had attended every town meeting, but one, held in the town for over sixty years. He was three times elected member of the general assembly. He always took an active part in church and society matters, and did his share towards their support. Mr. Barnard lived and died on the farm which he had commenced. He died in June, 1864, aged 82 years, and his wife died in 1870, aged 88 years.

J. J. Hapgood came to Peru in 1806, and received his education at the common schools in the town. He was a prudent, industrious, and calculating young man, and managed to save money from his earnings. In 1827 he bought the land in front of the brick hotel, which was almost a wilderness at that time, and built a small house, finishing half of the lower part for a store. This was the only store in the vicinity. Mr. Hapgood did a little in the potash business, and carried on the farm, while his sister attended to the store. In 1832 he married Hepsibah Barnard, who filled the place of housewife and clerk in the store. As time went on the business increased, and the farm, by hard work, was greatly improved. Mr. Hapgood erected all the buildings on his place. He always helped to bear the burdens of the church and society. He took the contract of building the new church, not including the foundation, for $1000, and finished it as agreed without any loss. With a little help from the society he put the new bell on the church. He also built the new schoolhouse at a very low figure, and he built the parsonage, above the cellar, for $400. Mr. Hapgood and his son Luke were connected in business under the name of J. J. Hapgood & Co., but sold out in 1870 to Snow & Co., who carried it on a short time and then sold it to J. J. Hapgood. Mr. Hapgood had partly filled the store with goods, when he died, and Marshall J. Hapgood then carried on the store for a time. The store was in the hands of the Hapgood family for about 57 years. Mr. Hapgood was a useful man, and used both means and time for the public good, and did more to keep up and sustain society during the years of his life than any other man in the town. He died in 1877.

In 1637 John, Joseph and Mark Batchelder came from Canterbury, County of Kent, England, and settled in Salem, Mass. Joseph Batchelder settled in that part of Salem known as Wenham, and his farm was situated near Wenham Pond, and has been kept in the Batchelder family through all the generations up to the present time.

John Batchelder, a descendant of Joseph, was in the war of the Revolution. After the war he married, and about 1783 moved to Mt. Vernon, N. H. His son, John, moved to Peru from Mt. Vernon in 1804, bringing with him his wife, whose maiden name was Fanny Hildrith. He began in the woods on the farm where his sons, Edmund and Hildrith, now reside, and built the first buildings on the farm. In 1823 he built the house that stands on the place at the present time. Mr. Batchelder was the second captain in the militia company, and was one of the two in the committee who built the first church in town. His wife died in 1819, and he afterwards married Nancy Barnard, who died in 1879, aged 92 years. Mr. Batchelder was deacon of the church from the time of his appoint-

DEA. O. P. SIMONDS

ment in 1834, until his death in 1855. He was about 76 years old
when he died.

Israel Batchelder came to Peru from Mt. Vernon, N. H., about
1808, his wife, whose maiden name was Abigail Wiley, of Amherst,
N. H., coming with him. He bought the farm, on which he lived
and died, from Marshall Bigelow, with a small house standing on it
in a clearing. Mr. Batchelder was elected justice of the peace, was
captain of the militia company, and was twice elected member for the
legislature. He died in 1858, aged 77 years.

Edmund Batchelder came to Peru from Mt. Vernon, N. H., in
1819, with his wife, whose maiden name was Betsey Jones, of
Amherst, N. H. They brought three children with them. Mr.
Batchelder bought his farm from Joseph Dodge, with a small house
and barn which stood on the place. He cleared the land and
erected all the buildings, and also built the wall. His wife died on
July 6th, 1869, aged 84 years, and he died on July 20th, 1869, aged
82 years, exactly two weeks after his wife. They had lived together
about sixty years.

In most respects the three Batchelder brothers were very much
alike. All had good farms and were good farmers, and they all had
their farms paid for. They had good buildings, and their farms
were adjoining each other. In the winter and on wet days they
worked at coopering, and in the summer they manufactured sap tubs
and butter firkins, for which they found a ready sale in the adjacent
towns. They had a thorough New England education, intellectually,
morally, and religiously. They all took great interest in having
good schools, and Edmund had been a teacher in his younger days.
They were members of the Congregational church, and did all they
could to sustain church institutions by their presence and means.
Edmund willed $500 to be kept by the church, the income to be used
for helping to support preaching. All three brothers took great
interest in town affairs, and were always willing to bear their share
of the burdens in supporting the institutions of the town. They all
three held town offices. They lived on their respective farms until
they died, each one leaving a son in possession of the homesteads.
These homesteads are still occupied by the Batchelders.

Deacon David Simonds came to Peru with his father in 1802,
being then about 16 years of age, and received a common school
education. He commenced clearing the forest on the farm south of
his father's place, meeting with all the hardships that the early

settlers had to contend with, besides which, his house was burned down. He was a man of reading and thought. Mr. Simonds and his wife joined the church in 1816. He was more of an Armenian than a Calvinist in his theological views, not a sectarian, but could fellowship with all who loved the cause of Christ. Mr. Simonds was an active deacon of the church for thirty years, and his mantle, as deacon, fell upon his son, O. P. Simonds, who is still in office. He was a man of mild temperament, and one who could take the prosperous side of life with ease, and the unpropitious side with submission. He believed in the freedom which our Declaration and Constitution proclaimed, and could not endure oppression in any place or person, country or race, black or white. Hence he early espoused the cause of emancipation, and labored with his friends to educate public opinion up to the standard of freedom and equal justice to all and for all. He lived to see his hopes fulfilled in his own country. Deacon Simonds died in 1869, aged 82 years, and his wife died in 1888, aged about 94 years.

Peter Dudley was the oldest son of Gen. P. Dudley, and was born in Peru, where he attended school, and sometimes taught the winter term. He married Delia Davis, of Londonderry, and lived in Manchester on the Gov. Skinner farm until his wife died. He then returned to Peru and bought the Nathan Whitney farm. About this time he married a lady from Royalston, Mass. Mr. Dudley sold his farm and bought the Tuthill place in Landgrove, but sold it again and bought the hotel in North 'Derry which he kept for several years. He next moved to Rutland, where he kept a hotel and had charge of a marble mill. Mrs. Dudley died in Rutland, and Mr. Dudley then moved back to Manchester. He married Sophia Vance for his third wife. Mr. Dudley was elected a regimental officer before he was of age, filling the place to the satisfaction of all and with honor to himself. He was a strong Democrat until the rebellion broke out, when his whole soul went into the struggle for the preservation of the union and the overthrow of slavery, and took just pride in the honorable part taken by his children. Charles P., his oldest son, went out with a three months' regiment, came home after his time was up and recruited for a company in Manchester, of which he was elected captain, being afterwards promoted to Major. He received a wound in the battle at Spottyslvania Court House, which caused his death. The second son was a lieutenant in the regular army. Norton T., the youngest son, died in prison in

Salisbury, N. C., in 1864. Mr. Dudley died at Manchester on January 10th, 1883, aged 80 years.

Gen. Stephen Dudley was the second son of Gen. P. Dudley, and was born in Peru on the 1st of June, 1805. He received all the education that could be obtained at the common schools, but being studious and eager for knowledge, his meagre school advantages were greatly assisted by reading. By these means he became a well informed man, and many who had far greater advantages were not so well read in the history of our own country and of Europe during the period of the first Napoleon's career. This prepared Mr. Dudley for useful positions in his native town, which, although it was Republican and he a Democrat, elected him as representative. He was also elected delegate to a constitutional convention, and often held town offices. He inherited a military taste from his father, and in 1840 received a commission as lieutenant-colonel of the 26th Vermont Militia, of which regiment he was promoted to colonel in 1842. In 1843 he became brigadier-general of the 9th Brigade Vermont Militia. The military spirit of General Peter Dudley did not all die out in one generation, for out of fifteen grandsons of military age, thirteen enlisted in the service, seven were officers, six were wounded, and three died in service. Gen. Dudley married Lydia Davis, of 'Derry, and spent his active life upon the homestead in Peru, where his ten children were born, of whom seven lived to grow up to manhood. Twins were born in 1835, died young; Myron S., born 1837; George B., born 1839, died 1863; Lucy, born 1841, died 1865; H. Elmer and H. Estelle, born 1843; Homer, born 1845; L. Caroline, born 1849; Stephen Guilford, born 1854, died 1866. Gen. Dudley sold his farm and moved to 'Derry, thence to Chester, and from there he went to Andover, where he died on October 21st, 1876, aged 72 years. His wife died about the same time.

Ira K. Batchelder, the oldest son of Edmund Batchelder, was born in Mt. Vernon, N. H., December 11th, 1811, and came to Peru with his father in 1819. He was educated at the common schools, with brief terms at the Chester Academy and at Teachers' Seminary, Andover, Mass. On coming of age he left Peru for eight or ten years, being engaged most of the time in teaching. After his return to Peru he taught several terms of school with great success. A native of Peru, and a prominent resident of Detroit, Mich., recently said, that his ideal of school teachers was best represented by Ira K.

Batchelder and Mary Simonds (Clark). Mr. Batchelder was for many years town superintendent of schools, and always had a most lively interest in their prosperity. From experience we know that the common schools in Peru from 1845 to 1860 were among the best in the state. In some of the select schools held in the town during this time the higher mathematics and languages were taught, and we could almost fit for college without going out of town. Much of the efficiency of the schools of that period was due to the personal attention of Mr. Batchelder. Besides, he took an active interest in everything that pertained to the welfare of the town, held almost every town office repeatedly, was very active and efficient in church work, and, last but not least, was the best farmer in town. He was appointed a justice of the peace in 1841, and has held that office up to the present time, a period of forty-nine years. He was chairman of the board of selectmen for eleven successive years during the war time. He represented the town in 1849, and was senator from Bennington County in 1850 and 1851, and associate judge of the County Court in 1864 and 1865. In 1869 he moved to Townshend, where he now resides. Mr. Batchelder has been one of the trustees of the Windham County Savings Bank for the past seventeen years. In 1840 he married Nancy, daughter of Benjamin Barnard, who has been his helpmate in all the circumstances of life, leading a more active life in the community where she lived than her husband. They were enabled to celebrate their golden wedding at their home in Townshend, March 12th, 1890. All their children, grandchildren, brothers and sisters were present, and with the help of the many friends that were present, a very enjoyable time was spent. Julia E., their only daughter, graduated at Burr & Burton's Seminary and at Mt. Holyoke Seminary. She married Rev. E. J. Ward, of Grafton, in 1867, and died at Grafton in 1872. She was a woman with noble traits of character, and her untimely death was greatly lamented. Their oldest son, James K., graduated at Burr & Burton's Seminary and at Middlebury College in the class of 1864. He studied law with the Hon. J. M. Tyler in Brattleboro, graduated at the Law School in Albany, and is now one of the prominent lawyers of the state. He represented the town of Arlington two terms, the last of which he was Speaker of the House. The youngest son, Edward, moved to Townshend with his father in 1869, where he is now engaged in farming, having one of the best river farms in the vicinity.

D. K. S.

George Batchelder was born in Peru in 1812, and received his education there. He worked on his father's farm until he was of age. About 1833 he went to Athol, where he served an apprenticeship at the carpenter and joiner's trade. He returned in 1837, bringing with him his wife, whose maiden name was Elvira Peck, of Royalston, Mass., and worked at his trade in Peru and the adjoining towns. He had charge of the work in building the churches at 'Derry and East Dorset, and the new Congregational church at Peru; he also finished the Methodist church in Peru. Mr. Batchelder served the town as constable, lister, selectman, and was twice elected representative. In 1853 he moved to Rutland, where he did some large jobs and had a good reputation as millwright. After a few years he returned to East Dorset, where he died in 1878, aged 66 years. His wife died about the same time. They left two children, Elsie, who married Duane Kent, of Dorset, and Theodore, who married and settled in East Dorset.

James L. Haynes, with his wife, one son and a daughter, came to Peru about 1855, from Fitchburg, Mass. He was a man fixed in his purposes; what he resolved to do had to be done, and what he did was done well. He bought the mill owned by Holland Tarbell, put it in good order, and turned out first-class work. Mr. Haynes's premises soon showed that a new man had taken possession, the land was cleaned up and made productive, and the highway was kept in good repair. Miss Haynes was educated for a teacher. She married Dr. E. P. Miller, who went to New York City and opened a retreat for the sick and infirm, which has proved a great success. Mr. Haynes's son, Charles, fitted himself for a teacher, and taught school for some time; he is now at the head of Miller's Hotel in New York City. Mr. Haynes died in Peru, and his wife then went to New York and lived with her children. In 1888 she came to Peru to spend her summer vacation with Deacon Edmund Batchelder, and died at his home. They were a family respected by everybody in town.

Aaron Burton came to Peru from Chester in 1835, and settled on the Bigelow farm. He was an energetic man, quick to decide and prompt to act. He changed all the buildings except the barn, and sold the barn over the brook. The shops were removed, and a new house built on the same site where the old one stood. Mr. Burton was a good farmer, and made great improvements in the land. He took great pride in having good horses and oxen. He was a good and useful citizen, and held many town offices. Mrs. Burton's maiden name was Susan Bigelow, and was a native of Peru. She was a good and useful woman, always ready to help and attend to those who were sick. Her mother, Widow Bigelow, lived with the Burton family until she died in 1861, aged 82 years. Mr. Burton moved to Manchester in 1862, and lived there until he died.

CHILDREN OF AARON BURTON.

Susan Abigail m. Mr. Chamberlin, of Manchester; he died. Her second husband was Dr. C. P. Hatch, of Peru; he settled in Acworth, and died there. She then married Charles Lyon; now living in East Salem, N. Y.

Bowman m. a lady belonging in Philadelphia, lived there. He was a bridge builder.

R. Bigelow m. Mrs. Johnson, lives in New York City.

Mary m. A. J. Gray, of Weston, lives in Iowa.

Lauren died young in Peru.

G. K. Davis, son of H. O. Davis, came to Peru with his parents, and received his education in the village school. He worked at farming until he became of age, when he spent several years in business in New York City. He returned to Peru with his wife and bought the Jesse Rider farm, which he greatly improved. After living on the farm several years, he bought the hotel now known as the Bromley House. Mr. Davis is a good hotel manager, and no one understands better how to get up a good dinner than his wife. Mr. Davis is an active man in town affairs, and has been constable longer than any of his predecessors, besides holding many other town offices. Although he was a strong Democrat, he was elected to represent the town in the general assembly.

CHILDREN OF G. K. DAVIS.

George m. Miss Johnson, of Wardsboro, lived in Derry, now in Lee, Mass.

Abbie Ann m. Mr. Pond, of Manchester, lives in Dakota.

Ida m. Hildrith Batchelder, lives in Peru.

Ezra P. Chandler, son of John Chandler, was born in Peru, and received his education in the district schools. He was a natural mechanic. At the time he became of age he had worked in different shops, learning to do everything that was needed to be done. In 1852 he built the house in which he lived, and later built a barn and large shop, which was well filled with tools, mostly of his own make. He made anything in wood that was needed, from a sap tub to a wagon wheel, also anything in iron, from a steel punch to a 4-horse engine. Mr. Chandler was a valuable mechanic to have in any community. He was a good citizen, and did all in his power to help society. He died in 1885, aged 55 years. Mrs. Chandler is still living.

Charles Lyon, son of Freeman Lyon, Sen., was born and educated in Peru. He worked at farming until he was of age, when he went to Hoosick and worked in a woolen factory several years. He returned to Peru and bought the hotel, but sold it again about a year later and went to Eagleville, N. Y., where he soon became partner in the firm of Cleveland & Lyon, manufacturers of woolen goods. He continued in this business until about 1869, when he sold out and bought the water privilege at Shushan, on which he erected a large factory, part of which was used for the manufacture of cloth and part for a grist mill. He carried on business in this mill until he sold out to his nephews, who had been working for him. Mr. Lyon has now become a banker, and is president of a National bank in Salem Village. He is probably the wealthiest man that was brought up in Peru.

Amos Batchelder bought the farm on which he resides from A. D. Lincoln in 1850. He is a native of Peru, and has always lived in town. Mr. Batchelder has always been a hard working man and a good citizen, willing to do his share in supporting the institutions of the town and society. He married Lucretia Jones, of Waitsfield.

CHILDREN OF AMOS BATCHELDER.

Edgar M. in Dorset, lives in Peru.

Ella M. Mr. Hewes, of Winhall, lives in Winhall.

Edmund M. Fannie Cross, lives on the homestead and takes care of his parents.

Charles J. works at lumbering in Peru.

James works on a farm.

The four sons are stout six-foot athletic fellows, and can do as much heavy work as any four brothers.

Harvey and Hezekiah Stone, sons of Joseph Stone, were born on the farm where they now live, and received their education in the town. They inherited the farm from their father, and have always lived on it, their only sister keeping house for them. They attend strictly to their own business, although financially, they stand among the highest in town. They are the only representatives of the large family which existed in town sixty years ago. Harvey Stone has been an active citizen, and has been often elected to important offices. He is a hearty supporter of the Methodist church.

Charles E. Barnard was born and educated in Peru. He married Harriet Holton, a native of Peru, in 1848. He came into possession of his father's farm, built the new house, and worked at farming and lumbering until 1864, when he sold out and went to Granville, Ill. He has been a very prosperous man, carrying on a large cattle business and owning more farms than any native of Peru that we know of. Mr. Barnard had a family of eight children, whose names are Frank, Fred, Mary, Anna, Ellen, John, James, and Hattie, who have all settled in the west.

Stephen D. Simonds, son of David Simonds, was a native of Peru, and received his education in the district schools. His wife's maiden name was Emeline Carter, of Jaffrey, N. H. In 1864 they, with their two children, George and Alice, emigrated to Granville, Ill., where they have been very prosperous. Mrs. Simonds died about 1867. Mr. Simonds married Ellen Stiles, of Peru, for his second wife, who died in 1890. His son George is doing a successful business as banker and lawyer in Kansas.

F. P. Batchelder, second son of Edmund Batchelder, came to Peru with his parents in 1819 from Mt. Vernon, N. H., and was educated at the common schools, with one or two terms at Chester Academy. He served an apprenticeship at shoemaking, and worked at his trade and at farming in his early life. Mr. Batchelder was constable for several years, and for a time was deputy sheriff. He was twice elected a member of the general assembly, and was doorkeeper in the house of representatives one session. In 1869 he sold his farm in Peru and bought a farm and milk route in Ludlow, which he run for several years. He then moved to Iowa, where he farmed to advantage for four years on a rented farm, after which he went to Dakota and bought a claim of 480 acres, proved it up and obtained a title. After building a house and improving the farm he sold out and went to St. Louis, where he is still living. Mr. Batchelder married Abigail Barnard, of Peru, in 1842, and they have five children, namely, Rosette, Mary Emma, Luella, Lizza, and Herbert P. All the children have settled west of the Missisippi.

James Bennett, son of Francis Bennett, came to Peru with his parents in 1819, and worked on his father's farm, attending school in the winter months. Soon after he became of age he married a lady from Boston. Mr. Bennett owned a piece of land, which he cleared

M. J. HAPGOOD.

himself and built a house. Five or six years later he owned and carried on the Samuel Stone farm, Deacon Wyman's farm, and Jesse Rider's farm. In 1840 he sold out and went to Rockingham, where he bought a store and carried on business about a year, then going to Boston and opening a provision store in partnership with his son Henry. They did a large business until 1880, when Mr. Bennett died. Henry still carries it on, under the name of Bennett & Rand. Jacob, another son, is doing a successful business in Philadelphia.

Deacon O. P. Simonds, son of Deacon David Simonds, was born in Peru in 1815, and with the exception of a year or two, has always lived in town. He built the house where he now resides in 1841. Mr. Simonds worked at the shoemaking business for over sixty years. He has served the town as town clerk forty-three years, and was twice elected representative to the general assembly. He has been a member of the church fifty-three years, and as deacon was present at all the meetings, generally leading the choir. Mr. Simonds married Mary Cone in 1839, and they had six children. They have lived together more than fifty years, and although their golden wedding was not celebrated, they were not forgotten.

Joseph H. Simonds, brother of O. P. Simonds, was born in Peru in 1818, and has always lived in town. He owned and lived on the farm which his father cleared, built the new house and improved the barns, and then sold it to Stephen Simonds. He next bought the farm where Albert lives, built a new house and barn, and lived on it until he died in 1876, aged 58 years. Mr. Simonds was a useful man, both in town and church affairs, being always ready to sustain any good cause by his presence and means. He married Emily Messenger, who is still living. Albert, his son, takes charge of the paternal acres, and is likely to fill his father's place in town and society. He was elected representative to the legislature in 1890.

Joseph P. Long came to Peru in his boyhood, and has lived in the town ever since. He lived on the paternal farm and took care of his father and mother. He was a prudent and industrious man, and erected good buildings on the farm, besides making great improvements in the land. Mr. Long held several town offices, and was twice elected town representative. He married Elvira Lakin, of Peru, and they had three children, whose names were, Madison, died in 1864, one son died young, and Henry, who is now living in Manchester. Mrs. Long died with consumption about 1855. Mr.

Long died about 1879. His second wife, who was Widow Lincoln, is still living.

Stillman W. Lincoln came to Peru with his parents, and received his education in the common schools, where he was always considered a good scholar. He was a man of great energy and activity. His wife's maiden name was Ann Whitney, of Peru, and she is still living. Mr. Lincoln bought the Francis Bennett farm, and lived on it until 1837, when he moved to Pittsfield, Ohio, bought a farm and improved it. A few years later he moved to Oberlin and bought in one of the best locations in the city. Mr. Lincoln died in 1882, aged 72 years.

Jacob Bennett, son of Francis Bennett, came to Peru in 1819, and worked on a farm until he became of age, attending the district school during the winter months. He went to Boston and worked in a store as clerk for several years, but afterwards went to New York and entered into partnership in a dry goods firm. Mr. Bennett was a good business man, and his prospects for success were very flattering. He died suddenly with cholera in 1829, aged about 26 years.

L. B. Hapgood was born in Peru in 1841, and received his education in the town. He worked in his father's store as clerk until he became of age, when the firm of L. B. & J. J. Hapgood was formed, in which he continued until 1870. He then went to Boston and entered into partnership with C. M. Hapgood in the wholesale shoe business, but was burnt out in the great fire. Mr. Hapgood is now foreman in the shoe store of C. M. Hapgood, in Easton, Penn., and has an interest in the business. He married Ellen Davis, of Peru, about 1864. Mr. and Mrs. Hapgood have been useful citizens wherever they have lived, and have always taken great interest in the prosperity of the church to which they belonged.

C. M. Hapgood, after his return from the war in 1864, went to Boston and entered a shoe store as clerk. He soon afterwards became partner in the business, but was unfortunately burnt out. After remaining in business at Boston a few years, he went to Easton, Penn. A company was there organized under the name of Hapgood, Hay & Co., and did a wholesale and retail business in boots and shoes of all kinds. Mr. Hapgood attended to buying the stock and had the general management of the business, which increased from year to year. The company was dissolved in 1889, but Mr. Hapgood continued in the same business, and is now doing a larger business than any other man who went from Peru. His residence is one of the finest in the town.

Mark B. Lyon, son of Joel Lyon, was born in Peru and educated in the district and select schools. He worked on his father's farm until he was of age, then worked some years at the marble business in Dorset, where he also taught school. Mr. Lyon married Abbie M. Rideout, of Dorset, and returned to his father's house. In 1869 he bought the best farm in town, on which he has proved himself a successful farmer. Mr. Lyon is a useful citizen and an active worker in the society and church of which he and his wife are members. He has represented the town in the legislature, besides being elected to several town offices.

J. C. Lakin, the only son of Capt. James Lakin, was born on the farm where he now resides, and was educated in the district school. His children have received their education and become teachers in the same school. Mr. Lakin is an active citizen, and has held many important offices. Although a strong Democrat, he was elected representative by the town. He married Elvira Rideout, of Dorset.

Charles Batchelder, son of Edmund Batchelder, was born on the farm where he now lives, and has lived there most of his life. His wife's maiden name was Abbie Davis. Mr. Batchelder, being the youngest son, came into possession of the ancestral farm, and he and his wife provided and cared for his parents as they passed down the declivity of life and crossed the Jordan to the new Jerusalem. Mr. Batchelder's sons have all left home, and he has carried on the farm alone for years. He is a good citizen, and always willing to do his share of any town business. Mr. Batchelder and his wife are liberal supporters of the society and church of which they are members.

Samuel Stiles, son of Capt. Francis Stiles, is a true blooded Vermonter, by birth, education, and practice, and by being quick to decide and prompt to act he has accomplished whatever he has undertaken. He came into possession of his father's farm, and has since added another farm to it, besides building a new house. His parents and grandparents lived with him in their old age. Mr. Stiles married Miss Conable, of Bernardston, Mass., who died; he then married her sister, who is still living. They are Methodists, and are active supporters of that church.

Dexter Batchelder, son of Israel Batchelder, was born at Peru in 1820, and was educated in the village schools. In 1841 he went Dorset and worked in Wm. Williams's tanyard. While there he married Susan Bloomer. After a few years he returned to Peru to take charge of the homestead and care for his parents in their declining years, a duty which he and his wife faithfully performed. In 1840 he bought the farm where his son Robert lives, repaired the house and moved on to it, converting the large house which stood on the homestead into a cheese factory. Mr. Batchelder took an active interest in town business, and was always ready to aid in any useful improvements. Although he was not a member of the church, he did a great deal towards the support of the society and institution of the church. He represented the town in two sessions of the legislature, and was one of the county judges at the time of his death. Mr. Batchelder died in 1888, aged 68 years. His only child, Robert I., inherits the estate.

D. K. Simonds, son of Deacon David Simonds, was born at Peru 1839, and spent his childhood and youth on his father's farm and at the district school in Peru. He went to Burr & Burton's Seminary to prepare for college, and graduated from Middlebury College in 1862. He then practiced law in the office of Crone & Bisbee, Newport, Vt., being admitted to the bar in 1865, at Orleans County, Vt. Mr. Simonds edited the Newport Express in 1865 and 1866, the St. Johnsbury Times in 1870, and for the past twenty years has been proprietor and editor of the Manchester Journal. He has been town clerk for eighteen years, was postmaster for eleven years, register of the probate court fourteen years, was elected representative from Manchester and senator from Bennington County. Mr. Simonds married Ellen Clark, daughter of Rev. A. F. Clark, of Brattleboro, who was a teacher of music at Burr Seminary.

Rev. Myron S. Dudley, son of Gen. Stephen Dudley, was born in Peru, and received the rudiments of his education in the common and select schools of the town. He fitted for college at Burr & Burton's Seminary, and graduated from Middlebury College in 1863. In 1863 he entered the army, joining the Veteran regiment as private, but was afterwards promoted captain. He was wounded in the battle of the Wilderness, and mustered out of service in 1865. Mr. Dudley then studied theology, and was ordained and settled at Chelsea, Vt., from which place he went to Cromwell, Conn. In 1890 he moved to Nantucket, Mass. He has been a useful man, and is greatly esteemed wherever he labors.

James M. Dudley, third son of Gen. Dudley, was educated at the district school, Chester Academy, and Burr & Burton's Seminary. He entered the office of Judge Washburn, in Ludlow, to study law, and remained there two years, then entering the Albany Law School, where he studied until he was admitted to the bar. Mr. Dudley associated himself with Horace Smith, a former classmate, and carried on business at Broadalbin. From there he went to Openheim, Fulton County. In 1855 he moved to Johnstown, the county seat, and formed a partnership with the late Judge Bell, which continued until the death of the latter. Mr. Dudley possesses a good legal mind, well disciplined by study and experience, and is felt to be a lawyer who can safely be trusted with complicated cases.

Deacon Edmund Batchelder, son of Deacon John Batchelder, was born on the farm where he now lives, and where he intends to live until he crosses the river, when his son Hildrith will take possession of it for life, and then leave it to his son. It is eighty-seven years since Deacon John Batchelder commenced on this farm. Edmund Batchelder married Sophia Simonds, who died in 1856, aged 41 years, and he then married Augusta Parker, of Putney, who died in 1867; his third wife, whose name was Mary (Rider) Fairbanks, is still living. Mr. Batchelder has been an active deacon in the church for thirty years, and has been a member about fifty years. He has been a member of the Sunday school seventy-one years.

A. T. Byard, only son of Aaron Byard, was born and educated in Peru. He married Jane McMullen, and they went to live on the paternal farm. Mr. Byard provided and cared for his father and mother while they lived, both of whom lived to be over ninety years of age. Mr. Byard improved the farm and erected a fine house. After his children left home he sold the farm and bought the Mark Batchelder place in the village, which he greatly improved, but afterwards exchanged it for the farm that Asa Phillips commenced on. He still owns this place, but resides in Townshend, Vt. Mr. Byard is a man respected by all, having been a good citizen and a useful member of the church. He represented the town two years in the legislature.

C. F. Long is a son of Isaac G. Long, who came to Peru from Londonderry about 1828. He was educated in the village schools, and worked on the farm with his father until he became of age. He then worked at turning chair stock, but it did not agree with his health, so he commenced peddling tinware, soon, however, changing that for dry goods, and did an extensive business. He bought a large farm in Dorset, improved it, and then sold out. Mr. Long then went to Detroit, Mich., and formed a company under the name of Batchelder & Long, to deal and work in stone. After doing a successful business for some time, he sold his share in the company and moved to Iowa, where he lived several years. He is now living in Ypsillanti, Mich. Although Mr. Long's health has always been delicate, he has been able, by care, to lead a very active life, and has been successful in all his undertakings. He married Martha Batchelder, of Peru, who died in 1888, aged 58 years. Mr. Long is a liberal supporter of society, both by his means and presence.

Edward Batchelder, son of Israel Batchelder, is a native of Peru, and spent his youthful days on his father's farm. At maturity he went to Massachusetts and worked in different shops. He married Harriet Wyman, of Peru. Mr. Batchelder then bought the Ballard mill and run it a short time, selling out to Gustave Albee. He next worked as a wheelwright, and afterwards bought the brick hotel, which he run about a year and sold to G. K. Davis. Mr. Batchelder was a useful citizen, and besides being elected to many town offices, represented the town in the legislature two years. He moved to East Dorset, and is now foreman in D. L. Kent & Co.'s marble mill. After Mr. Batchelder's first wife died, he married Widow Vials, of Dorset.

Jonathan Hapgood, son of Josiah Hapgood, was born in Peru, and spent his early days in the village. He did his life's work on the farm where he was born, caring for his father and mother in their old age. He married Aurelia (Davis) Marsh, of Reading, Vt. Mr. Hapgood built the new house and made great improvements on the farm. He was a man who worked for the improvement of the institutions of the town, and held many important offices; he was also elected to represent the town two terms. Mrs. Hapgood died in 1882, and Mr. Hapgood in 1883. They were living at their son's residence in Manchester when they died, but were brought to Peru for burial.

James H. Wait, son of James Wait, came to Peru in childhood with his parents, who settled in district No. 6, in 1835, and which was an unbroken wilderness at that time. He assisted his father in clearing the farm during the summer months, and attended school in the winter, where he soon proved to be a good scholar. He learned the joiner's trade, and has always worked at it. Mr. Wait married Nancy Wyman, daughter of Thomas Wyman, and settled in East Dorset, where he built a house. He was always an industrious man, and one who enjoyed his prosperity.

John W. Davis, son of Grovenor Davis, came into town with his parents when he was four years old. He received his education at the common school of the district in which he lived. When quite young he commenced peddling tinware, but finally moved to Manchester, where by perseverance and industry he soon had a large business. Mr. Davis married Betsey Roby, of Peru. The business is now carried on under the name of John W. Davis & Son, and deals in tinware, sheet iron, stoves, lead pipe, and all kinds of goods kept in such establishments.

Henry Davis, second son of Grovenor Davis, received his education at the school in district No. 6, and worked on his father's farm until he became of age. Early in life he commenced running Thayer's hotel at Factory Point, but left it in a few years and moved into the Colburn House, where he run a popular hotel for about twenty years. Mr. Davis retired from the hotel business with the credit of being a popular landlord.

Six sons of Goodell Walker, whose names are John G., Ira R., Seth L., Duane, Merrill G., and Peter J., were all born in Peru and received their education in the village schools. They worked on the farm with their father until they were twenty-one years of age. All of them married and first settled on farms in Peru, John G. being the first one to break the ring and leave town. He has lived in several towns, but has spent most of the time in Peru, and has owned different farms and dealt in real estate. Ira R. has lived on several farms, but for more than twenty years has occupied the house where he now lives. He married Catherine Wyman, of Peru, and had one daughter, who died when quite young. Seth L. bought the Dudley farm, and has lived on it ever since. All the large buildings were struck by lightning and burnt down, but better ones have taken their place. He married Mrs. Abbie Drury, of Weston, who died in 1889. Duane married Irene Stoddard, of South 'Derry. He died in 1863, aged 30 years, and is the only one of the six brothers who is dead. Merrill G. married Rosette Stiles, of Peru. He owned several farms in town, the last one being the Bigelow place, on which he built a fine house. He finally bought a farm, saw mill, and jelly factory in

Manchester, where he is now doing business under the name of M. G. Walker & Son. Porter J. came into possession of the paternal acres, which he sold and moved to Manchester, where he built a house. He is now doing business for himself in Inglewood, Ill. All the six brothers were industrious and useful citizens, taking an active part in town affairs, and holding offices at different times. John twice represented the town in the legislature. They all helped to support society, and were members of the church. Merrill G. and Porter J. were active members in the church and Sunday school, and their help was much missed by the society.

Of the large family of John H. Sawyer, only two are living. John married in Massachusetts, and then went to California, where he has prospered. Sarel, the third son, after the death of his father, entered into an engagement with his mother and the heirs to remain on the farm, take care of his mother, and pay a small sum to the heirs, which he did until he came into possession of the homestead. He re-built the saw mill, put in new machinery, and otherwise improved the premises. Mr. Sawyer is a man of great muscular power, and has done a good deal of hard work on his farm. He married Jane Conable, of Bernardston, Mass., and has three daughters, all of whom are married.

M. J. Hapgood, son of J. J. Hapgood, was born at Peru in 1849. He attended the village school, and then went to Burr & Burton's Seminary to prepare for college. After he had finished his course at Williams College, he studied in different law offices and attended lectures at the Harvard Law School, afterwards being admitted to the bar. Mr. Hapgood commenced business with the firm of J. J. Hapgood & Co. in the mercantile store at Peru, and continued in the business for a number of years. He entered the lumber business, bought large tracts of land, and erected a steam mill on the mountain, which has done a large business. Mr. Hapgood does more to support society and the institutions of the town than any other citizen.

Of the six sons of J. W. Farnum who were born and brought up in school district No. 4, David is the oldest. He married Miss F. Burton, of Manchester, and went to live in Herndon, Va., but now resides in Maryland, where he has prospered. Aaron, the second son, was suddenly killed by the bursting of a stone in a grist mill at Arlington, Vt., leaving many friends to mourn his loss. Henry, the third son, married Miss Benedict, and resides on the farm formerly

occupied by Mr. Benedict in Arlington. He is a useful citizen of
that town. Charles E., the fourth son, married a lady from New
Hampshire, and is settled in Washington, D. C., where he is a
master builder, with an extensive business. Lycena, the fifth son,
married a lady at Peru. He moved to Arlington, and is doing well
at farming. The sixth and youngest son is married and settled in
Dorset. The oldest daughter, Miriam, married Edwin S. Simonds,
and lives in Herndon, Va. Mr. Simonds holds an office at
Washington, D. C. Amanda, the other daughter, married Frank
Rand and lives in Townshend.

James Farnum came to Peru about 1835, and married
Remembrance Long. He owned several farms in town, but the
latter part of Mr. and Mrs. Farnum's life was spent with their son,
where they both died, aged about 73 years. Charles, the oldest son,
married Maria Carlton, and lived on various places until about 1865,
when he purchased the Killam farm, on which he is doing a good
business. He has a family of girls. Wallace, the second son,
married Miss Estabrook, of Manchester, and has always lived in
town. He now owns the Aaron Byard farm, and is a successful
farmer. Fayette, the third son, married Miss Simonds, of Peru, and
settled at Manchester Depot. He is a mechanic, and is doing
a successful business. These three brothers are industrious men and
good citizens.

LONGEVITY.

Widow Sarah Killam Stiles was the oldest person who ever lived
in town. She died in 1868, aged 102 years and six months. Her
one hundredth anniversary occurred on Sunday, and was celebrated by
holding a meeting at her residence and uniting with her in celebrat-
ing the Lord's supper. Rev. M. A. Gates officiated. Her mind
continued bright and clear almost to her last days.

In the family of Reuben Bigelow there were eight daughters
who grew up to womanhood in Peru, and were as follows. Abigail,
died in Chester in 1888, aged 92 years; Susan, died in Manchester
in 1868, aged about 70 years; Lucinda lives in Illinois; Demietta
lives in Illinois; Deborah lives in Michigan; Laura lives in
Wisconsin; Orrilla and Caroline live in Virginia. The combined
ages of the sisters that are alive is 503 years, which averages 83½
years each.

NAMES OF THOSE OVER NINETY YEARS.

Sarah Farnum, 92; Lucy Wood Barnard, 97; Mrs. John Batchelder, 92; Mrs. Joel Adams, 95; Widow Lovina Hapgood, 97; Aaron Byard, 95; Mrs. A. Byard, 95; Mrs. Abigail Long, 93; Mrs. Sally Farnum, 95; Jesse Brown, 92; Mrs. Sally Cook, 94; Mrs. Anna Simonds, 94; Mrs. Peter A. Gould, 93; Ebenezer Stiles, 92; Mrs. Scammel Burt, 92; Parker Wyman, 91; Widow Sarah Messenger, 96.

NAMES OF THOSE OVER EIGHTY YEARS.

Mrs. Benjamin Williams, 82; Mrs. Joel Lyon, 84; Peter A. Gould, 82; Mrs. J. L. Haynes, 80; Horace Gould, 80; Mrs. Elijah Simonds, 84; Daniel Wood, 83; H. O. Davis, 82; Polly Stone, 83; Oliver Wyman, 85; Deacon Seth Lyon, 83; Dana Wyman, 83; Joel Adams, 82; David Simonds, 83; Moody Roby, 88; Asa Farnum, 86; Stephen Tuttle, 83; Deacon John Davidson, 84; Widow Stratton, 87; Zimri Whitney, 86; Jesse Brown, 87; Mrs. Zimri Whitney, 82; David Robbins 85; Mrs. Lydia Walker, 82; Moses Rider, 86; Mrs. Asa Simonds, 80; Freeman Lyon, 80; Mrs. John Brown, 87; Elisha Whitney, 84; Freeman Lyon, 2nd, 80; Benjamin Barnard, 87; Mrs. Reuben Bigelow, 83; Mrs. Deacon Lyon, 87; Stephen Bennett, 84; Mrs. Jesse Brown, 81; Edmund Batchelder, 83; Mrs. Edmund Batchelder, 84; Mrs. Isaac G. Long, 84; Mrs. Asa Farnum, 82; Benjamin Barnard, Jr., 82; Mrs. Benjamin Barnard, 88; Mrs. Stowell Barnard, 82; Mrs. John Brown, 87; Mrs. Stephen Bennett, 82; Mrs. David Robbins, 87; Moses Adams, 85; Stephen Tuttle, 83; Mrs. Ira Russell, 80; Elijah Simonds, 85; Mrs. Daniel Wood. 83; Mrs. Elisha Whitney, 81; Jane Taft, 80.

www.ingramcontent.com/pod-product-compliance
Lightning Source LLC
Chambersburg PA
CBHW031956060726

47497CB00016B/2316